The Well Travelled Road

Short Stories & Poems

Brian Grehan

Published in 2010 by New Generation Publishing

Copyright© Text Brian Grehan

First Edition

The author asserts the moral right under the Copyright, Designs and Patents Act 1988 to be identified as the author of this work.

All Rights reserved. No part of this publication may be reproduced, stored in a retrieval system, or transmitted, in any form or by any means without the prior written consent of the author, nor be otherwise circulated in any form of binding or cover, other than that in which it is published and without a similar condition being imposed on the subsequent purchaser.

Dedicated to Deirdre,

My beginning, middle, and end.

Acknowledgements

I would like to thank my wife *Deirdre*, without whose ongoing encouragement, this book would not have happened.

Also the members of *The Long Table Creative Writing Group*, for their expert advice and help.

And my good friend *Bob McCabe* for his fine sketches.

And Se Murphy for his invaluable computer expertise in getting the book to production stage.

All proceeds from this book will be donated to charity.

Contents

An Egyptian Message	7
A Walk in the Park	17
How's That?	27
Two Cities	33
A Family Matter	41
It's Not Cricket	53
A Roman Picture	63
Day and Night	75
Freedom	89
Goodbye	103
Holy Orders	109
Mindin' the Kids	119
The Wedding	129
Belief	139
Cuban Song	149
A Faraway Place	159
Decision	167
Reconciliation	181
Survival	195
That Time of Year	207
The Hunt	227
The End	233
The Well	239
The Mountain	243
Famine Grave	245
Eastertide 2005	247
Altar	249
Autumn Thoughts	251
Freewheeling	253
Over the Moors	255
Yes, I Will	257
Two Angels	259

Requiem for a Shop	**261**
Pompeii Days	**263**
Years in Love	**265**
Alone	**269**
Artist	**273**
From the Holy Mountain	**275**
Like the Sunflower	**277**

An Egyptian Message

It was late February in Dubai, and the booming cannons proclaimed *Ramadan* had just ended its forty days of prayer and fasting .The traditional Muslim holiday of Eid had commenced. After my first year working with an Arabic family business conglomerate, the idea of a short break was appealing.

My wife Angela and I had dinner that evening with friends who had holidayed the previous year in Egypt. After a few drinks, and puffing cinnamon- flavoured hubbly bubbly pipes, we spoke of the possibilities of visiting Cairo, and the Nile Valley.

"Yes Jim, an unforgettable experience, but not always a pleasure." Paul said.
"First there's the food. Everyone gets a"gyppy" tummy there! Hygiene is abysmal. And then there's the people. Begging, pickpockets, poverty, and corruption everywhere. Bring lots of small change with you, and avoid carrying big money. An honest man is hard to find in Egypt! Still you must go, if only to see the Pyramids along the Nile!" My thoughts went back to an old Jo Stafford song that seemed to express that sentiment.

"Well thanks for that, we'll think about it. By the way, an honest man is hard to find anywhere. Scarcer than hen's teeth!" I replied.

Later that night we discussed again the idea of a short holiday in the land of the Pharaohs. The idea both excited and worried us .The previous year a busload of tourists had been massacred in the Valley of the Kings at Luxor by Islamic fundamentalist extremists .In the end, Cairo and the Pyramids, and cruising down the historic Nile, and viewing the famous royal tombs and ancient cities won out. In spite of a slight sense of foreboding, we booked the next day.

The day before we departed, I was approached by Abdullah, the oldest brother in the family business where I worked. Abdullah had previously been the Manager of an Islamic bank, which the family controlled, in Northern Cyprus. He was a kindly man, honest, and devoutly religious.

"*Eid mubarak*. Jim, I believe you are going to Cairo tomorrow, and I would be most grateful if you could do something there for me."

"*Eid mubarak*. Of course Abdullah, very pleased to oblige. What would you like me to do for you?

"If you would bring with you a message. It's a small parcel. It will be collected at eight o'clock tomorrow night at your hotel by Mishal, who was my accountant at the bank in Cyprus. It's very confidential, you understand?"

"Sure Abdullah. *Mafi miskala*. No problem. Is there anything important in it?"

"It's just some money. Mishal knows the details."

A wave of panic shot through my body.

"How much money would there be?"

"*Inshallah*, maybe twenty thousand dinar."

I quickly computed the amount as well in excess of thirty thousand pounds. My mouth felt dry inside. But I knew that under Arabic custom I could not refuse the request. I would be betraying the trust he had placed in me.

"Ok, Abdullah, I am honoured by your trust."

"*Hamdilillah*. Wonderful. I will bring it now."

He soon returned with a small brown parcel. I found it hard to believe that its value could be so high. It could easily fit into a lady's handbag. I returned quickly to the villa, my head spinning, with the parcel in my hand.

"Angie, it will only be for one day, but we must make sure that we never let this parcel out of our sight. Even on the plane."

"Ok, we'll keep it in my handbag always. It will be perfectly safe there."

"Good idea! There's no honesty in Egypt. They'd slit your throat for the price of their next meal!"

On the plane, Angie kept the handbag tight in her grasp. We were surprised to see many Arabic men entering the toilet on the plane in their white flowing robes, to emerge minutes later dressed, in smart, western suits. As the plane descended on Cairo the early morning sun evaporated the mists along the Nile to reveal the Pyramids, studding the desert sands like giant black teeth.

We were uneasy at the large number of security guards at the airport, all carrying Uzi submachine guns.

Leaving Cairo airport we had to tip four people separately to get our luggage onto the taxi. Just as we had been forewarned, the Egyptians swarmed like vultures onto the rich pickings of the tourists arriving in their country. The poverty of the people was immediately visible. They all seemed to have a desperate look in their eyes. It was the law of the jungle. Survival of the fittest.

The city of Cairo was like a dragon, seething and devouring people in its flaming jaws. Pollution poured from its streets, overcrowded with dilapidated Russian built cars. Piles of rubbish could be seen burning in side streets. Flies buzzed around the dunghills, and cats prowled the refuse heaps. Raw sewage could be seen spewing into culverts in some side streets. Overcrowding was so bad that in one area, known as the *City of the Dead*, people lived in the crypts and mausoleums of an ancient cemetery. There was just too many people living there.

The rising sun broke the pollution haze above the city, as donkey carts clattered along the streets, oblivious to the honking cars surrounding them. A beautiful young girl, carrying a small baby in her arms, weaved between the slow-moving, fuming cars, selling roses. I bought one through the open taxi window. *What kind of a place is this, that a beautiful young mother is reduced to begging in such appalling conditions to survive with her child?* Yet in spite of the chaos around them, the people seemed happy and smiled a lot.

We passed a museum honouring the glorious six day war against Israel in 1967. Outside a warplane was mounted high on a stand. Nearby was a statue of Nasser.

Strange, it was the first time I'd ever seen a country commemorating a war it had started, then lost.

The taxi driver's name was Mohammed. He was a tall, handsome man with a dark moustache and aquiline nose. He was charming, with good English, and kept the conversation flowing. He said his elderly mother lived with him, and he had six daughters to support, along with his wife, and her mother. I wondered if this was the truth, or just a ploy to get a bigger tip.

We hired Mohammed for the rest of the day, and after checking into our hotel, headed off to view the Pyramids. Angela kept her handbag safely in her hands all the time. We both agreed that whatever one said about Cairo, the Pyramids redeemed everything. Breathtaking. However, everyone there was hustling for money. Even the Government and army staff would break the rules for a few dollars.

"It's ironic Angie, the Pharaohs ripped off the people, made them build the Pyramids to preserve their immortal remains, stashed them full of fantastic treasures, and later the people plundered the tombs, and took back what was originally theirs ."

"Yes, I suppose everything goes in circles. But what a magnificent edifice to a monumental ego! Anyway, I think we should get back to the hotel. I don't feel at all safe here with my handbag stuffed with money."

Mishal was calling to the hotel at eight o'clock to collect the money, so we showered, changed, and went for dinner at six in the main restaurant. Angie kept her bag safely under the table beneath her feet. After a fine dinner and bottle of wine, we both began to relax. A cabaret act started in the restaurant, and soon a nubile belly dancer swayed around the tables to pulsating drum rhythms. She sat on my knee while Angie took a photo. I pressed her palm with a tip before she glided away, inclining her head in thanks. I looked at my watch. Seven. The waiter, who had been excellent, brought the bill. We decided to give a generous tip in cash into his hand later when leaving, and paid the bill by credit card. I then ordered two brandies to round off the meal. Exotic Egypt was starting to cast a spell over us.

    A short time later there was a din out in the foyer. I went to investigate. An Egyptian wedding was taking place in the hotel, and the beautiful bride, resplendent as an Egyptian Queen, in flowing dress and golden jewellery, was descending the stairs with her father, to the music of the grand march from 'Aida', played by a live orchestra. Huge spotlights lit up the scene, which was being filmed. I rushed in excitement back to the restaurant.

    "Quick Angie, you must come and see this before it's finished. It's spectacular. Like a royal wedding."

    We raced back to see the final minutes of the entrancing spectacle. Just when the music had stopped, a thought struck me like a bolt from the blue.

    "Angie, the handbag?"

    "Jesus, it's back in the restaurant."

    We raced back to the table. Gone. I felt a hollow feeling in my stomach. A feeling of disbelief at what had happened. Unfortunately it was not a dream, but the realisation of our worst fears.

"Jim, I'm really sorry, it's all my fault."

"Don't be ridiculous, I called *you* out to the foyer. Let's keep cool. It's bound to be here somewhere." I replied with a confidence I certainly did not feel. Panic was very much setting in.

We asked people at adjoining tables if they had seen the handbag, but they had all been watching the finale of the cabaret act. The waiter had cleaned off the table and was no longer on duty. The money would be ten year's salary to him. I also began to think what I would say to Abdullah. My career was finished. Over one stupid mistake. I had betrayed the trust bestowed on me. I would never be able to live it down. I would have to make good the money, which would wipe out any savings we had made in coming abroad. Not to mention the rest of the holiday would be ruined. I began to feel part of an unreal nightmare. I tried to stem the feeling of desperation and terror growing like a cancer in my stomach. Stay calm and keep looking. I checked my watch. Half an hour to Mishal's arrival.

A thorough check of the restaurant revealed nothing. I spoke to the receptionist, who was unable to help.

"Angie, I'll have to see the manager, and report the theft. And bring in the police. For all the good either will do." We were both now resigned to the inevitable.

I made an appointment to see the hotel manager, and fifteen minutes later walked into his enormous office on the fifth floor. Mahogany panels on the walls and ceiling. Persian carpets on the maple floor big enough for a dancehall. Behind the large square desk sat the manager. Inscrutable like a Sphinx. He was thickset, with bushy eyebrows, dark hair and suit. He held a large cigar in his stubby fingers, which were covered with rings. He was surrounded on either side by an assistant, also dressed in a dark suit. I felt intimidated by the room and the people. The manager stood up.

"Please be seated. Jamal Ashari at your service. Can I be of assistance to you?"

"My wife lost her handbag in the main restaurant in the hotel tonight."

"What time did this happen, and what was the colour."

"About seven o'clock tonight. It was white."

"Would this be the handbag?" he replied, opening the top right hand drawer of his desk and placing a white handbag on the desktop. It *was* Angie's. I held my breath and tried to stay calm.

"Yes, it appears to be my wife's. May I examine it?"

"Of course. Please do."

I slowly opened the bag, heart hammering. I saw the brown parcel inside. Intact.

"Mr.Ashari, I can't thank you enough. You don't realise what this means to my wife and I. Where was it found?"

"Under your table in the restaurant sir. Your waiter Mahmood immediately handed it in. All our staff are highly trained in honesty and customer service. This is a Trust House Forte hotel."

I thanked the manager again profusely, and left a very generous tip for the waiter, which made the manager raise his eyebrows in surprise, and rushed back to break the good news to Angie. We hugged each other in delight.

"Somebody up there must surely like us, Jim. To have found an honest man in Cairo. It's like finding buried treasure in a tomb!"

"Yes, I guess we should never jump to conclusions."

Ten minutes later we met Mishal in the lobby and with great relief handed the parcel over to him. He gave me a receipt and said.

"Thank you so much for safely bringing the money. You Irish are very reliable and trustworthy. In this country it is impossible to find an honest person. One you could trust."

"Yes Mishal, you're probably right in general, but I'm sure there must be someone out there who would not let you down."

He just smiled politely, as he turned and walked out the door.

A Walk in the Park

It was just another Monday morning. Nothing special. Peter Logan yawned, and looked out his bedroom window, the only weather forecast he trusted. April showers. Well, what else this time of year? At least the daffodils should be out this week. He sometimes felt that without his ritual walk with Monty, he would have had difficulty getting up every day.

It wasn't always that way, he mused. When Joan was there beside him, it was so different. *Everything* was different. He would make the breakfast for her, and sit by the bed as they ate, and chat about things. And laugh. He loved that. He still saw her long dark hair flecked with grey and hazel eyes under dark lashes. And her smiling, laughing face. But that's all in the past. Got to stop thinking about the past. That's what the doctor said. That's what they all say. Think about the present, and plan for the future. Yes, I must do that, he thought. But,what future? A dog's whine cut through his thoughts. Monty was up and looking for his breakfast.

"Monty, you old rascal, getting you from the Rescue Home was the best thing I ever did. You know you were only five days from taking the Long Walk." he said, as he placed the dish on the floor, and ruffled the dog's ears. It was actually Joan's idea to get a dog, he recalled. He had taken early retirement from the Bank eight years ago. He was fifty years old then, with twenty five years service. It was not altogether an amicable parting. He was bitter at not getting more appreciation, and promotion, over the years. "Should have licked ass, like the others who got on, even though they didn't have a clue." He said to himself. Still, it was a good package, and with their son and daughter both in relationships, and fled the nest, it was the perfect opportunity for them to enjoy life together.

And Monty was one of the first things they did when he retired. Medium-sized, brown, with big, floppy ears. He was named after a dog his beloved grandmother in Carlow had, many years earlier. And the daily walk in the park became part of their life. Until two years ago. Just a routine check-up for a small lump on her breast. The doctor said everything should be all right. But he was wrong. Dead wrong. And the worst outcome imaginable. All in six weeks. Got to stop thinking about the past. But how? And her second anniversary in just two weeks.

A headline in the Sunday paper caught his eye. *FEMALE JOGGER ATTACKED IN PARK*. He picked up the paper and read the article. A jogger in her thirties had been set upon in a park near Cabinteely the previous week. She had beaten off the attacker, and escaped, but the assailant was still at large.

"We better keep a sharp eye out today, Monty. There might be a reward going." Peter said, as he dangled the lead over the dog. Monty barked in anticipation, his tail wagging like an up-tempo metronome.

As he sauntered with Monty down the road to the Park, he remembered his promise to Joan to always continue the daily walk. She said she would like that. He wondered if he would hear the cuckoo today. She always became excited when she heard it. She said it filled her with hope for the summer ahead. He suddenly realized that for the past two years the walk was the main social event in his life. He had met so many good people with dogs of all shapes and sizes. He looked forward to their daily conversations. His kids were always at him to get out of the house more, and socialise. But apart from playing Bridge once a week, he had so far avoided other social contact. He didn't like going to the pub, and usually spent a few hours each day in his garden to fill the void. He liked reading, and listening to classical music But was he, he asked himself, just avoiding situations for a quiet life? As he had done in work all his life. Should he be more assertive and outgoing? There was a woman he had met recently at Bridge that he had found attractive. Her name was Mary Summers. But she was married, although she came to Bridge every week without her husband. He had partnered her one night at the club, when his usual partner was ill. They had got on very well, but it was only later that he realised he rather liked her. He heard also that her husband had a serious illness. I should have been more forward, he thought, I might never get the chance again. Ah well, that's the story of my life.

   The park ablaze in yellow and green, his spirits lifted at the sight of the sun dancing on the banks of daffodils, beneath the bare giant oak trees, in amongst the snowdrops and crocuses. There was birdsong in the air. But no cuckoo. He bade good day to Mrs. Mooney, who waddled by with her Lurcher, named Prince. Mr. Allen was taking his two enormous Irish wolfhounds out of his four wheel drive. A large lady with a beaming smile passed by, with four dogs of mongrel breeds, and nodded in his direction. The last time he spoke to her, she had told him that some of her best friends were dogs. He guessed she was a professional dog walker. Then he saw a tall slim, fair haired woman jogging towards him, with a white poodle in tow. She was wearing a grey track suit, her hair tied back in the breeze. As she came near he saw her black almond eyes, and recognized Mary Summers.

She stopped beside him, taking the Walkman from her ear.

"Mary, what a surprise. I didn't know you had a dog, or that you jogged in this area."

"Hi Peter, yes I like to have a run every day. I do a number of different routes. Sometimes, it's Dun Laoghaire pier. Sometimes Killiney hill. I like to vary it around a bit to avoid the boredom of running. That night we played Bridge together, you mentioned that you came here everyday, so I thought I'd like to try out a new route." She replied, smiling, with her head tossed back, breathing deeply, arms akimbo.

"And your dog?"

"Yes, Fifi, isn't she cute? Your dog seems to be taking a fancy to her." She laughed, as Monty began sniffing around Fifi's tail." I read about that jogger being assaulted here last week, and thought a dog would be some deterrent. Hence Fifi."

"Great. You'll never regret it. Dogs are great companions. They take you as you are. But I'm not sure a dog her size would scare off any attacker." He replied laughing.

"I can assure you, she can be as feisty as any female when she wants. My husband Pat will vouch for that."

"And how is your husband? I understand he's not been well lately."

"Not good, I'm afraid. He's in a very weak condition. He's had a number of minor strokes over the past few years. He had to retire early from the civil service. Unfortunately it's been progressively downhill ever since." She sighed, rubbing her eye. "Social life is zero, I'm afraid. You don't tend to get invited anywhere when you're alone. That's why I started jogging."

I know the feeling, he thought. Only too well. As he listened to her, he gaze took in her slim and well-shaped body, and when he ended on her dark almond eyes, he knew then what really attracted him. Like two deep dark wells.

"Yeah, that's really tough. I'm very sorry to hear that. Is there any hope of an improvement?"

"Not really, but you live in hope." She said, as she started to put the Walkman back into her ear.

"What kind of music do you listen to?" he enquired.

"Classical always. Pat and I used go to the Concert Hall every week. But that was a long time ago. I really miss that. See you at Bridge on Thursday, Peter. Come on Fifi." She waved, and as she moved gracefully away the dappled sunlight lit her hair in a golden light.

Like the daffodils, he thought, as he released Monty from the lead. Fancy her liking Classical music. He had gone many times to the Concert Hall with Joan. He should have asked her to go with him. What's wrong with that? Nothing. To hell with what people say or think. We're two mature adults. Anyway, she probably would have said no. He consoled himself with that. But he'd never know would he? Yes, he should have been more positive. Like Monty was with Fifi. Well, maybe not that much.

"When it comes to the opposite sex, I should take lessons from you Monty." He said, as he walked towards the path corner, guarded by a row of swaying poplar trees.

"Put that effin mutt back on the lead, or you'll pay me an on the spot fine here and now." snarled a short stocky man, dressed in black uniform and cap, stepping from behind a poplar tree, notebook and pencil in hand.

Peter was startled, and before he could reply Monty uttered a low growl, and with hair hedgehog bristling on his neck, and teeth stripped right back, moved menacingly towards the warden. He had never seen Monty behave like that.

"Get that damned mutt under control, or I'll have him put down for aggressive assault, and you fined as well. All dogs must have leads in this Park from today. No more fouling and polluting here. I'm here to clean up this place." The warden snapped.

Peter was so taken aback; he immediately put Monty's lead back on, and headed on down the path. As he looked back, he saw the warden had a pair of binoculars around his neck, and a small green van was parked nearby in the bushes. Minutes later, reflecting on the incident, he became indignant at the warden's aggressive manner. Especially to Monty. He should have fought back. Been more assertive. Like Monty. No, he wasn't going to let that little twerp walk roughshod over him. He retraced his steps, went up to the van, and knocked on the window. It slid down.

"See here, I don't accept your accusations about my dog fouling this Park. That's my responsibility, and I always fulfil my obligations. We've been coming here for years. Your language to my dog was aggressive and abusive. I want an apology."

"The only thing I'll give you is a promise to do everything I can to have that mutt put down. You've just signed his death warrant." The warden spat back." I have eyes everywhere in this Park." He wound up the window, and put the binoculars to his eyes.

As Peter turned, he saw Monty relieving himself on the back wheel of the van. Good on you, Monty, he muttered to himself. Next it'll be dogs in nappies. He walked on and sat down on the next park bench, and reviewed what had happened. The second confrontation hadn't worked out as he intended. In fact, just the opposite. He was worried that he had put Monty in real danger. Signed his death warrant. No doubt the man was vindictive. There was real venom in the words he used. What a stupid thing to have done. Another shambles. He could go elsewhere. But his promise to Joan. No. He held his head between his hands for several minutes.

He continued the walk, but even the sun bursting out occasionally from the racing clouds, onto the golden daffodils, failed to remove the gloom. Monty, unfazed, was enjoying himself, smelling squirrel scents on the path, and barking at scavenging magpies. That cheered him a little. As he was coming back near to the entrance, he scanned the Park with his pocket binoculars. He hoped to spot a rare red squirrel, but instead saw the green van parked behind a large rhododendron bush near the river. He decided to check it out, and found a closer vantage point, approaching silently from behind. Inside, he saw the warden puffing a large cigar, and occasionally lifting a small bottle to his head.

   Peter yanked open the van door, and held his breath as the cigar smoke, and   whiskey smell hit him.

   "Smoking and drinking in the workplace! Definitely a dismissible offence. I'm a retired Garda officer. I know the score!"

   The warden was shocked. Peter could see beads of perspiration on his brow. His eyes bulged, and mouth dropped. After a long pause the warden spoke:

   "Look mister, I know I was a little hard on you and your dog earlier. I've been under pressure, since my mother died a few months ago. My friends say I've been acting strange ever since she died. I just can't get over it. The only way I can relax is to have a drink and a smoke. You've got to understand."

   I do understand, Peter thought. Yes, I do. If you only knew. He paused, before replying:

   "OK, I accept what you say. Anyway, I like to give everyone one last chance. Maybe. And you? Let's say if you're prepared to be nice to me and my dog, I'll be nice to you. And maybe forget what I've just seen. How about it?

   "OK. It's a deal. Let's shake on it" The warden quickly replied, shaking visibly, and extending his hand.

Peter accepted the handshake, and muttered in a low voice." Just remember, I don't tolerate anyone crossing me in a deal. I have photographs and a witness to prove my case." He was surprised afterwards how easily he lied.

He slammed the door shut, and continued until out of sight of the van. There was a spring in his step now, and he suddenly felt everything was going right in his world.

"We showed him, didn't we Monty?" he said scratching behind the dog's ears.

He was still thinking about the encounter, when Mary Summers re-appeared around a bend. She looked agitated.

"Mary, still running? I thought you'd be well gone by now."

"No. I was actually going to do two laps around the park, when I saw this green van, hidden behind some trees. I could have sworn there was someone inside, with a pair of binoculars. I suddenly thought of the stalker, and ran back this way. I was heading for the Garda station. I'm so glad I met you" she said, gasping.

He could see she was distressed from the experience.

Mary not only relaxed, but fell around laughing, when he related his story.

"Thanks Peter, for stopping me from making a fool of myself, and for saving Fifi and me from falling foul of the warden, although I can sympathise with his problems."

"It's nothing. Say Mary, I was wondering if you would like to go sometime to the Concert Hall. We both like classical music, so it seems a shame not to. But I do understand if you can't, because of Pat." There he'd finally got it out, even if it sounded damned awkward.

Mary looked surprised, and her eyelashes arched, as she pondered her reply.

"That's very nice of you Peter. I thought you were the shy, retiring type. But after today, I was obviously mistaken. Pat is always telling me to go to a concert with someone else. I presume he meant another lady. I'd like to think about it. Why don't we meet here again for a walk in the park, tomorrow? Fifi seems to have taken a shine to your dog anyway. What's his name, by the way?"

"Monty is the name. Yes, we'd both like that. It's a date. See you tomorrow. "

They parted and as he and Monty came to the park entrance, a shower spattered the pathway in front of them, and the wind suddenly gusted. And then he heard it. The cuckoo's double barrelled cry rang out clearly in the wind. And again. And again. He smiled to himself, and continued walking out the gate.

How's That?

My earliest years were spent in depressed, post war Dun Laoghaire, long past the glory days when it was known as Kingstown. We lived on the main street, and the clanging trams, with their comet trail of sparks overhead, stopped outside our front door. We played on the streets. There were no playgrounds or playing areas. Not many today either. Roaming around in gangs it was cowboys and Indians in the "gut" at Salthill, or hide and seek behind the beached buoys beside the green in front of the harbour, or watching the steam trains shunting at the station.

My older brother and I had no regrets when our family moved to Blackrock in the early fifties. We were both crazy into sport, and the new council house had a large green outside, where every sport imaginable was played at all hours and in all weathers. It was the Promised Land! Except for certain narrow-minded neighbours, who were always watching through the curtains, waiting for a ball to land in their garden? In a flash they would dash out to grab it, and put an end to the games on the green.

In school we played Rugby, although most of the teachers were Brothers and preferred Gaelic games. Brother Butler stood out from the others. He was fanatical about the game of cricket. He would regale the class about the state of play in the current Test Match between England and Australia. And how Len Hutton had scored a century or Freddie Trueman had taken five wickets in an innings. The other thing that set Brother Butler apart was that he never used the leather in class.

He used incentives instead to get results. Ahead of his time! He would divide the class into teams for all his subjects, each with a captain. The winning team got a prize, usually a bag of sweets. He got the best results, and we all looked forward to his classes.

In our religious classes we were told that anyone not of our religion, that is a Protestant, had little chance of getting to heaven. You almost thought they were going around with horns protruding from their heads! You were warned about even putting your head inside the door of a Protestant church! Near the green in front of our new house was a small shop, which I visited all the time. The shop was frequented daily by the pupils of a nearby Protestant school. They used it as their tuck shop. The pupils wore a brown school uniform, and I never saw any horns protruding. In fact they were really friendly, and would sometimes share their sweets with us, or give us a few coppers. The school was famous for hockey, and played cricket and athletics in the summer. It had wonderful playing pitches. Flat with grass like Wembley stadium.

After a few years in our new house, I found a Walter Hammond cricket bat hidden away in our attic. It belonged to my father, and was at least twenty years old. My brother and I then started a series of "Test Matches" on the green. Amazingly, everyone wanted to play, even kids who had never played before! Maybe it was the game itself, or the fascination of holding a real cricket bat in their hands that attracted them! Anyway cricket on the green soon became a popular summer event, and each year we slowly improved our performance with bat and ball.

The problem with playing cricket on our green was that after the activities of the winter, it was bare right up the centre, and it did detract from the game's enjoyment. One summer evening, our wicket-keeper Bernard, who lived opposite the Protestant school, said

"Hump this for a game of soldiers. Let's take up the stumps and go and play in the school across the road. There's nobody there in the evenings. They won't mind. Let's take a chance."

We all agreed, knowing deep down we would be trespassing, but the lure of playing on a real cricket surface won out. We gathered our bat, ball, stumps, and bails, and our motley crew of local village urchins headed across the road to the school grounds. The forbidden fruit.

It was beyond our wildest dreams. A real cricket pitch, marked out perfectly, with creases, and even holes for the stumps. The pock of leather on willow, and the ball zinging over the crew-cut grass to the boundary! Heavenly. A few of the boarders in the school, who were practising athletics gave us quizzical looks, but generally ignored us. The Test Matches then began in earnest. We played until dusk each evening, and sometimes continued well into the dark. As the word got around more kids came across the road to play in the fabulous surroundings.

About three weeks later on a fine June evening, we were in the middle of a practice match for the upcoming "Test" series, when we heard a commotion and looked around to see a large gathering of school pupils entering the gate to the playing fields, headed by the Principal, Mr. Parker.

"The game is up. Let's skedaddle outta here." said Bernard, whipping up the stumps.

We all legged it as far as Acre's field, fully expecting the Gardai to be right after us. For some reason we stopped there, and agreed we should go back and face the music. After all they knew where we came from, so there was no point in running away. We turned back and saw that the large crowd of pupils had stopped in the middle of the field, and that Mr. Parker and one of his senior pupils, were continuing alone in our direction. It was quickly agreed that my brother and I go and parlay with the enemy, and get the bad news over as quickly as possible.

We were too nervous to say anything. Mr. Parker did the talking, his glasses glinting in the evening sun.

"My pupils have asked me to come and talk to you. I understand that you all live across the road. I am delighted to see that you want to play cricket. It's a wonderful game. You are very welcome to come here as our guests anytime you wish to play. You may also borrow the school's cricket equipment for practising, including wicket-keeping and batting gloves, provided you return them every evening. And you can practise in the cricket nets. My only request is that you do not interfere with any of the school pupils who are using the grounds for athletic activities, and you do not use a wicket marked for a schools cricket match. And finally, I would like to arrange a full cricket match between Avoca School, and your team next Saturday week. By the way, does your team have a name?"

"Tha…. thank you very much Mr. Parker, we will do as you ask, and we would love to play a real cricket match with the school. We call ourselves the "Castlebyrne Owls" Cricket Club, because we're always playing in the dark." I replied, feeling overwhelmed by his generosity of spirit. Nobody could believe it when we relayed the good news back to our gang. We felt we had been let out of jail.

We duly turned out for the match on a scorching day, dressed in whites for the first time, had tea on the lawn, provided by Mrs. Parker, and crowned a memorable day with a victory in the match. And every year from then on we played a cricket match with the school, and it was the highlight of our youthful summers.

Two Cities

It was June '91 and the first Gulf War had ended three months earlier. On the plane journey to Arabia, John Kent read an article by the famous Middle East writer Robert Fisk, describing the Iraqi army retreating in disarray from Kuwait, four months earlier.

The beaten Iraqi soldiers had fired the oilfields and commandeered any available vehicle and headed up the main highway to Baghdad, led by the armoured vehicles. Out of the cover of the black toxic clouds rising over the inferno of the oilfields the US planes easily picked off the leading tanks, which blocked the vehicles behind. The red desert sand blushed a deeper colour from the blood of the dead and the highway became a mass of screaming bodies and flaming, twisted metal. The scorching sun was hidden as the smoke and flames reached up to join the poisonous clouds over hanging like a black shroud... Even the desert vultures stayed away.

He stepped off the plane in Riyadh airport glad that the war was over. The Scud missiles had been his big worry. He knew they had a range of three thousand miles. He was a vet and had taken up a two year posting with a large Irish Dairy Company in Arabia.. He had felt in a rut in Ireland. Life had become boringly predictable. A change is as good as a rest, he thought, and this is a chance to see the world, experience new challenges, and then home again. And the money wasn't bad.

He recalled the night they broke the news of their departure to their parents. He showed them a company video, portraying a very favourable image of life on the Arabian Peninsula, with private villas, sunshine and swimming pools etc. When the video was finished, he spoke to his mother:

"Mother, we're going there to live for a few years, what do you think?"

"I'll say a prayer for you son."

"What do you mean?"

"I don't trust the Arabs"

"Why?"

"They always carry a dagger in their stocking!"

Annie's mother was more positive and replied

"Great, when can I come and visit?"

As the summer climate in Arabia reached up to 140 degrees there was a mass annual exodus to cooler climes, and it was agreed Annie would not travel until September.

The week before his departure they spent a long, romantic weekend in Paris. Their favourite city. The hotel was small but their room had a fine view of the nearby *Eiffel* Tower. They took the Bateau Mouche at the Pont Neuf and alighted at Notre Dame, visited Shakespeare & Co., strolled up the Place St Michel into the beautiful Luxembourg Gardens, and sat and watched la Vie Parisienne.

"Annie, this city is probably the absolute opposite of where we're going"

"In what way."

"It's beautiful, liberal, and romantic."

"You're right, it's a tale of two cities, but let's make the most of it now, especially the romance"

And they did.

The first thing to hit him on arrival in Arabia was the opulence of the magnificent King Khalid Airport. It was palatial, with cascading water descending mosaic steps onto an enormous fountain. He felt he was in a fantasy world. Reality quickly set in when he went through the customs and security check-ins. After a two and a half hour wait, during which every person's belongings were meticulously scrutinised, he finally exited the building; but not before several magazines he had brought were taken away, and returned with advertisements for ladies lingerie blacked out with a felt pen. He felt tolerated, but not welcome.

The company's HR Manager, Kevin Connell, briefed him on his first day at work on the rules and customs of the Kingdom.

"John, you have to understand the two big "mortallers"here are alcohol and women .You cannot publicly or privately drink alcohol, or be found in the company of a woman who's not your wife. Immediate expulsion from the country, or *worse*, is the punishment."

He soon discovered the first taboo led to a huge "home brew" industry in the housing compounds. The second meant single people had to be very discreet or lead very boring lives.

He also learned that women had to wear in public a full length silk dress, called an Abiya which also covered their heads, leaving only their eyes visible. He noticed how alluring a woman could be when all you could see was a pair of large brown flashing eyes crowned by black, curved eyelashes, or maybe a beautiful ankle on top of a gold stiletto heel. The rest was left to the imagination!

Arabia also had a religious police, Mutawa, trained and paid to ensure that the religious laws of Islam are obeyed. They were extremely zealous, and hung around shopping malls hassling western ladies who had their heads uncovered. They also ensured shops were closed, and vacated, during prayer times. They also spied on Western expatriates and expatriate housing compounds to detect anything which could be against Islam's religious beliefs.

He was very impressed by the people's faith and belief in God, or *Allah*. They prayed five times a day, called *Salah,* facing Mecca. The prayer call, *Allah Akbar*, God is great, boomed out on tannoys throughout the city calling Muslims to the mosque.

The social life improved immeasurably when Annie arrived, and soon they were looking forward to their first trip home. The month before their holiday coincided with the holy month of *Ramadan*. Unfortunately there was a mosque outside the compound close to their villa. During *Ramadan* the volume on the tannoy was increased several decibels. Every night for the whole month their sleep was interrupted by the *Imam's* wailing voice reciting readings from the holy *Koran*. As the holy month was reaching its conclusion the moaning voice was building up to a screaming crescendo each night, reaching a climax on the final night when they hardly slept at all. Work had also been difficult for John, due to an outbreak of foot and mouth disease on a farm. He was feeling the pressure.

"God, Annie I really am looking forward to the break, I feel stressed out."

"Me too. Why don't we stop a few days in Paris on the way home? To unwind. It's April and everything will be lovely. Paris in the spring. Flowers blooming in the *Luxembourg Gardens*. Boats on the *Seine*. How about it?" You'll relax you in no time."

"Great idea, let's do it ".

The night before they travelled they drove to the gold *souk in Riyadh,* located in an area called *Baatha*, near *Chop Chop Square*, where people are beheaded Friday morning, to the cheering of up to one hundred thousand people. The *Mutawa* were very prevalent, so they completed their shopping quickly; buying some gold jewellery, paintings, a couple of novelty alarm clocks with a prayer call awakening, a camel stool, some *bedouin* jewellery and masks, and some copper pots. Despite the fabulous wealth of the city, the traders there were very poor, but had a great dignity and humanity, as they prayed with their worry beads moving nervously in their hands.

At last they arrived back in Paris, to their favourite hotel beside the Eiffel Tower. Their room with a view of the Tower was booked, so they parked their bulging suitcases in a room on the other side of the hotel. They lay down for a few hours rest after the long journey. After a short time they were awoken by the prayer cry of *Allah Akbar*. John jumped up with a start.

"Jesus, Annie, we came here to get away from this. There must be a mosque nearby. The *Muslims* are even taking over Paris!"

He rushed downstairs, and demanded to be moved to another room. After checking that other room was quiet, they had their luggage transferred.

They spent the afternoon visiting the *Marais* district in the Jewish Quarter, and saw the early spring flowers in the *Place des Vosges*. After a fine meal that evening in an art deco restaurant near St Michel, they returned to the hotel. They began to feel again the romantic mood of Paris. It was eleven o'clock, and John opened the window and saw the *Eiffel Tower*, lighting the Paris night sky in front of their room. Suddenly the sound of *Allah Akbar* rang out again. John felt a lump rising in his throat. "They're everywhere" he muttered. But the sound seemed now to be coming from over their room. They traced it to an air-conditioning vent high up on the wall. He stormed down to the reception desk, and in a loud voice explained his frustration.

The young German manager was quite sympathetic, and leaned over the desk, saying confidentially:

"Yes, you are right monsieur, they now have mosques all over Paris, and I have heard that they even put tapes of the *Koran* into the air conditioning systems in hotels to spread the word of their religion around the hotel rooms."

"Really? You think they could have done that?

"Perhaps, monsieur, I will come to your room immediately."

The young manager entered their room, stood on top of the unopened suitcase left against the wall beneath the air conditioning vents, and listened. There was no sound.

"I will have the maintenance engineer come to your room tomorrow and open up the vents to check inside properly. I am sure we will get to the bottom of this mystery, monsieur."

When he had left, John spoke

"At least he agrees with us about the spreading of the *Muslim* faith, because I thought initially he might think we were a little crazy. In fact I was wondering if we were both freaked out."

"Don't worry; he's obviously taking the matter quite seriously".

About an hour later, John, who was reading a book, suddenly jumped up

"Annie, I've just had a terrible thought".

And with that he rushed to the bulging, unopened suitcase, under the air conditioning vents, that the manager had stood on, and pulled it to the centre of the room. He quickly opened it, and rummaged in it, until he found what he was looking for --- a bag containing two cardboard boxes. Opening the boxes he took out the two novelty alarm clocks that they had bought in Riyadh, which emitted the *Allah Akbar* prayer call for the wakeup call. He remembered the person selling them had set the alarm on each when he was testing them in the shop. He checked the times that the alarms had been set for. It was exactly the same times that they had been hearing the prayer call in the hotel!

They thought of the young manager, and the maintenance engineer coming, and suddenly they both fell on the bed laughing until their sides ached.

"We had better be out when the engineer calls. If I tried to explain, we'd both be locked up".

And as they continued laughing, the veil of anxiety they felt under began to lift like a cloud, and for the first time in a long period, they began to feel completely relaxed, and gazing out at the *Eiffel Tower,* the magic of Paris began to wash over them.

"It's a tale of two cities, darling, and we're in the romantic one, so let's make the most of it."

And they *did.*

A Family Matter

Peter Hudson left his chambers in the Four Courts, and guided his BMW into the Friday evening traffic snarl in Dublin. He had endured a hard day in Court with a cantankerous Judge, and the weather forecast for the November night ahead was grim.

He was the eldest son, and heading for a family meeting, which he had convened with his two brothers and sister, in Killiney Castle Hotel, on the southside of the city. As he drove slowly to the hotel the storm clouds were gathering, and he felt strangely edgy about the evening ahead. There hadn't been a social gathering in the family since their mother had her first stroke three years ago. His relationship with Mark, a doctor, and James, a priest, had faded over the years. He wondered, in Mark's case was it sibling rivalry, or the close relationship of their wives, who were twin sisters, or the fact that he had been appointed Executor of his mother's will. His sister Louise also felt aggrieved that she had sacrificed the best years of her life to look after her mother, while the boys, in her view, had avoided their responsibilities in the matter. He didn't like to think too much about Louise's griping, but deep down a feeling of guilt haunted him. The week coming was also the tenth anniversary of his father's death, and that added to his foreboding.

The sky was menacing. A clap of thunder overhead shook his confidence as he drove through the hotel's castellated gates. Staccato hailstones bounced off the windscreen. Dashing from the car, lightning crackled the leaden sky into an eerie glow. He was relieved to reach the sanctuary of the hotel.

The rectangular room was sparsely furnished. Two narrow windows overlooked the car park. A round table covered in a green baize cloth, overhung by a crystal ball. Four wooden chairs. A large pitcher of water and four glasses. None of the finer comforts. He had made sure of that. It was going to be that kind of night.

Everyone arrived promptly and after a few minutes of stilted conversation, Peter decided to get the ball rolling:

"Thank you all for coming, on such a hellish night. I'll cut to the heart of the matter straight away. Basically we're here to discuss mother's health. She's really gone downhill fast, since being transferred to the hospital. The last time I saw her, she hardly recognized me. She's being drip-fed, and is now on a ventilator. "

"Peter, I hope you've not brought us here to play God with our mother's life." said James accusingly, his fingers straightening his white collar.

"Good heavens no, James, why would I do that, especially as you're here as God's representative? We're here to air our opinions about what's best for mother. After all we owe her so much for what we have achieved in our lives. We owe her a big debt."

"She owes *me* a big debt. In fact you all owe *me* a big debt." exploded Louise" I gave her five of the best years of my life. And what have I got to show for it? You all had your own lives to lead, and I was left alone to look after mother. I love her, but she could be very demanding and manipulative, and she suffered personal problems. It wasn't easy."

"We do appreciate what you've done for the family, Louise "said the Priest "God will reward you in due course. But you're not exactly on the shelf, are you? You're still a fine looking woman, and you'd make a great wife and housekeeper for someone."

"And what would *you* know about getting married?" She snapped back, tears of frustration welling in the back of her glittering, hazel brown eyes." There are other things in life besides marriage."

"Indeed there are." Peter quickly added, trying to divert the conversation, and noting that while Louise was still attractive, with wiry blond curls, she had lost that bubbly sense of humour of her early twenties. And there was the trauma of a four year old relationship breaking down in her mid twenties, just when they were all waiting for the wedding bells to ring out. *And* the rumour of an ongoing relationship with an older, married man.

"We need to get back to the main event. I've had a long meeting with her medical team, and also visited mother. She's in a semi-vegetative state. She can't hear or speak, but I did detect a glimmer of recognition in her eyes, but I can't say if she understood any of what I spoke to her. There are tubes protruding everywhere. It's very depressing .The fact is that the cost of maintaining her present treatment will have serious financial implications for the family."

"Ah, so it's finally out, it's all about money, you're equating our mother's life with money!" Mark, the doctor finally spoke, agitatedly." It seems strange coming from you, a legal beagle living in your detached Foxrock mansion, with your fancy yacht on display in Dun Laoghaire marina, and your children attending the most expensive schools in the city, that medical costs maintaining your mother's health, should be an issue. Father would turn in his grave."

"At least I *have* children, Mark, and I make no apologies for what I have. Everything I own, I've worked hard to get." Peter immediately regretted his knee-jerk reply.

"Everyone has the right to life. The Church is quite clear in this matter. I wonder if I could order a drink, Peter." The Priest's interjection defused the immediate confrontation, and Peter was quite happy to change the conversation.

The Polish waiter left a tray containing a bottle of Scotch, and a Vodka and tonic on the table, and politely left the room.

During the ensuing lull, Mark spoke again.

"Anyone mind if I light up? I'll leave the room if necessary."

"You have my blessing. But stay here, you wouldn't send a dog out on a night like this." James replied." In fact, I might join you."

"Would someone *please* open the window a little?" Louise interrupted.

A few minutes later, after knocking back a quick scotch on the rocks, Peter felt the knot loosen in his stomach. He looked up and saw the crystal ball covered in a haze of blue smoke. Like the ring around Saturn. Distracted, he uttered his next words without thinking.

"Mark, it's always fascinated me to know why Doctors smoke. It seems against everything you're trying to achieve in your profession."

"I honestly don't know, Peter. There are some things you do in life that don't make sense. Like last week you were seen with a bit of skirt, good looking too, in a Dublin hotel restaurant, while your wife was away for a break with your kids in Galway." He smiled in satisfaction to himself at sinking the knife deep.

"I think you're mistaken there, Mark. That was a client, and I can prove it. *Rumour* and innuendo don't count in court."

Mark's mobile interrupted. He excused himself and stood up.

"An appendix? No. Sorry Gary, I'm in the middle of something. A family matter. Can't leave now. Ring Gerry Peacock. For fifteen hundred, he'll do the job."

"Finished Mark? It's good to see even the medical profession have a price on everything. What about the Hippocratic Oath? Or should I call it the Hypocritical Oath?" Revenge is sweet, Peter thought.

"In the name of God, let's get back to the reason for us all being here. What have you got to say about mother?" The Priest exclaimed in a loud, frustrated voice, banging the table with the now-half-empty whisky bottle, which was now residing beside his glass.

"Relax Padre; I know it's difficult for you these days, with no new vocations to relieve the strain, and numbers dwindling in church attendances. Must make you sometimes feel like Jesus. *Rejected* .And of course there's the sexual scandals, and the cover-ups. Not a good example to us sinners. Go easy there on the drink." Peter again realized it hadn't come out the way he intended, but having started, he stumbled on.

"The reality is that father's money has run out in paying the nursing home bills. Costs have sky-rocketed since mother entered the hospital. The house will have to be sold. Even that will only cover the expenses for three years."

"And what about *me*?" cried Louise." It's *my* home. I can't afford to rent on the pittance a Social Worker gets paid. And after all I did in looking after mother all these years. It's not fair. You guys should all put your hands in your pockets. You can afford it. And you owe it to mother."

There was an uncomfortable silence. She had hit the nail precisely where it hurt.

"That's what we're here to discuss. You have to decide what is living. I wouldn't want to live if my quality of life is that of a vegetable. The days of miracles and Lazarus-like recoveries, and all that mumbo-jumbo we were fed in school, are dead. "Peter continued, feeling more confident and relaxed after the whiskey.

"And what about the recent recovery of the young man from death's door? The one called the "Miracle Man." And the Church's teaching on euthanasia?" The Priest retorted, as he raised another glass to his mouth.

"Well, he was in his early thirties, and age is a big factor. As for *euthanasia*, everyone knows it goes on everyday in hospitals, but not officially. Many deaths are due directly to overdoses of pain-killing drugs to treat the medical problem, usually at the behest of the patient's family, who wish to alleviate their loved one's distress. Is that not so, Mark?" Peter cleverly deflected the matter into the medical domain.

Mark paused a few moments before replying." No. I *don't* accept the tenor of your statement, but I cannot comment any further due to confidentiality considerations, and the laws of medical etiquette."

Well ducked, but you're not getting away that easily, Peter thought, before continuing, and playing his ace.

"As you all know, I am Executor of mother's will. The way things are heading this will be a very simple affair, as there will be nothing left, when all the medical and nursing bills are met. There *is* a potential inheritance of a million from mother's older, unmarried sister, who is seriously ill in Canada. What I would like to do now is read you a *living will letter* given to me by mother when she entered the nursing home. She asked me to read it to all the family, if her health seriously deteriorated. I think we have reached that point now, and I'm going to read you the contents of this letter, in accordance with her wishes."

"Well, it's *unusual* to hear a person's will wish before she's dead." Louise exclaimed, interestedly.

It may not be what you all expect to hear, he thought, before opening the envelope and commencing to read.

"My Dear Children,

I love you all dearly, and equally, and thank you for all the happiness you have brought to my life. Especially you Louise, who have given me so much of your time. I hope you find a good man, as I did, to love and look after you. But keep away from married men. They'll promise you the stars, and leave you gazing at the moon. I'm sure your brothers will ensure that you keep the house, after all your hard work looking after me.

And you James pray for me, as I do for you always. Yours is a lonely, solitary life, so be careful with the drink. It's been the ruin of many a good priest. It's a pity you can't marry. Even Jesus had Mary Magdalene. But I suppose the Pope, and his entourage in Rome are going to make sure that if they didn't have any fun in their lives, then neither will you.

To Mark, and Peter, you both have my best wishes for the rest of your lives. You have both done so well, and I hope you will always stay close. Mark, I hope that you will be blessed with children. With all the modern drugs, you more than anyone should be able to make it happen. And Peter, who is always so perfect, who has it all made, don't make a fool of yourself, and your family, by fooling around. You'll pay for it in the end.

Since Father died my life has been an empty shell, and I long to join him again. It is not my wish ever to live on as a vegetable, artificially supported by new-fangled medical machinery. In my view, that's not living. I want to die with dignity. If I reach such a state of health, it is my dying wish that you do not prolong my life any further. Please understand how I feel, and follow my last wish.

   Your Loving Mother "

   There was a stunned silence in the room, and the wind wailed crazily outside through the open window. Peter was gut-wrenched, and went to pour another whiskey, but the bottle was empty. Mother, always in control, he thought, even to the end. He gathered himself again, threw the letter onto the table, and continued.

   "Well I think you all have clearly got the message on mother's wishes. All I can assure is that she was in full mental control when she handed me the letter. What we need to do now is have a full family agreement on whether we agree to carry out her wishes. For my part, I'm happy to accede to her last request. And what about you, Louise?"

   Louise hesitated, wiped her eyes, and slowly replied."Yes, I agree."

   "And you James?"

   "My heart says yes, and my soul says no."

"Then I take that as an affirmative. And finally, you Mark?"

A lingering pause ensued, while Mark stood up and paced the floor, become finally replying.

"*No*. I cannot accept that this is the right course of action. In fact I am surprised at your ready acceptance of this letter. Either she was *non compos mentis*, or she was put up to signing a letter, without knowing the contents."

Peter felt his heart pumping like a piston, but before he could reply his mobile rang. He left the room, and returned quickly. His face had turned pale, and his voice was barely audible, when he spoke.

"It was the hospital. Mother has just passed away in the last few minutes. They said it was a peaceful death. She seemed content and quietly slipped away in her sleep."

Another dead silence ensued, broken by James.

"I will look after the funeral arrangements. She will be re-united with Father. It will be a private, family affair."

"Thank you James. That would be fine." Mumbled Peter, reeling from the shock.

A short time later, Peter shuffled out the hotel door. It had stopped raining, and the pale moonlight lit the car park like a searchlight. Passing a large pool of water, he looked down and saw his reflection mirrored below. He was startled to see a dark figure resembling Death the

Messenger staring back at him. An uneasy shiver flickered through his body as he unlocked the car door.

Seated inside he felt better, and as the car slowly started to move, he flicked on the radio. The sound of John McCormack singing "*I Hear You Calling Me*" came over the airwaves. It was his mother's favourite song, and he had once heard her singing it for his father, many years ago. A wave of emotion hit him, and he felt tears streaming down his face. I can't remember when this last happened, he muttered to himself, as the hotel faded in his rear-view mirror.

It's Not Cricket

It was London in the early eighties; and it wasn't exactly swinging. Or so thought Donald McGuire, as he switched off the TV in his comfortable Marble Arch apartment. Another pit closed down today in Lancashire. Four hundred more jobs gone west. I suppose Maggie Thatcher is delighted. Another score for her in her crusade against lame ducks! That woman, she's a legend in her own head, he thought, as he picked up the newspaper, and switched on the radio. *Bright Eyes*, Art Garfunkel's big hit filled the room. At least rabbits are not an endangered species, he muttered to himself. Unlike English industry! It seemed as if the *Iron Maiden* was determined to drive a wedge between the industrial North and the prosperous South. Between the workers and the gentlemen. Like the House of Commons and the House of Lords. And the Players and the Gentlemen in cricket. A divided country indeed! If they do this to their own, it's just as well the Irish split years ago.

He glanced at the weather forecast for the coming May Bank Holiday weekend. Cool with scattered showers. Typical bloody early cricket season weather! He had just been sent to London by his new English employer on a month's training course to their Head Office in the West End. Completely over the top! As if he didn't know how to sell textiles! After the first week he was feeling homesick. He rang his girlfriend Angie every night. What a bore! And he was missing the beginning of the cricket season with his club in Malahide; where he was captain of the third eleven. Angie won't be complaining, he mused; at least she won't have to make the teas! He hoped to take in a few cricket games in London to relieve the tedium. Great, he murmured, as he saw Middlesex were playing Somerset in a one day game on the coming Sunday at *Lord's*. Things are looking up!

Sunday morning dawned dull and dank. An early lunch in a fast food café, and he was walking up Baker Street towards St John's Wood. The clouds were lifting a little in the grey sky, and he felt a tingle of excitement as he passed the Gold Mosque and swung left towards *Lord's* Cricket ground; the Mecca of the cricket game. A damp chill still hung in the air. A two sweater day, he thought to himself.

Before filing through the turnstiles, he stood and admired the beautiful wrought-iron gates. Dedicated to W.G.Grace, the greatest English cricketer of all time. The Master. The venerable doctor's image, complete with bushy beard and cap was emblazoned in the centre, with a brief history of his unrivalled career underneath.

Inside, he was awed by the grandeur, and sense of history of the grounds. The Long Room, at the rear of the pavilion, he knew, had a famous cricket museum. The prize exhibit there was the *Ashes*; a tiny urn which contained the cremated remains of the stumps used in the first Test Match in which Australia triumphed over England at the Oval, over a hundred years earlier. Since that time it has been played for every two years by the two countries; and never has such a tiny trophy caused such excitement and controversy. Particularly in 1932 in the famous *Bodyline* series. In order to overcome the awesome batting of the young Aussie prodigy *Don Bradman*, the English team and management devised a strategy of packing their side with fast bowlers, and bowling at the batsmen's body instead of the wicket. England won the Ashes, but they were accused of unfair play. *Bradman* went on to become the greatest batsman in the history of the game. Donald then remembered with pride that his father had told him that he had been called after the great *Bradman*; who was his father's hero.

   He sat looking towards the famous Warner Stand, crowned by the weather vane of *Father Time*, scythe in hand, removing the bails from a set of stumps. The long wooden seat was damp, so he folded his raincoat as a cushion and sat on it. Low clouds scudded above the grey apartment blocks dwarfing the ground. The sun refused to appear, but it was dry and the players were limbering up on the pitch. The ground was sparsely populated, when the captains tossed, and it was announced that Somerset would bat first.

   A large gentleman in a cap and beige overcoat sat beside him as the opening batsmen made their way to the crease. A few minutes later a tall, thin man with a limp, dressed in a mackintosh, sat on his other side. This man had grey hair, and a thin moustache under a reddish nose.

   There was a hush over the crowd, as Donald watched the huge West Indian fast bowler Syl Clarke, walk slowly back, measuring his run up for the opening over. After 25 strides, he placed a white marker on the ground, and began a series of stretching exercises. Finally, after pawing the ground like a charging bull, he lumbered into a gradually accelerating run up to the bowling crease, and in a whirling windmill of arms and legs, unleashed an express delivery in the direction of the batsman. Donald gasped. So did the crowd. He never saw the ball, it travelled so fast. Neither did the crowd. Neither did the batsman as his off stump catapulted out of the ground, and the bails sailed high in the sky. An excited buzz started in the crowd as the batsman forlornly trod the long walk. A golden first ball duck! He had never seen such fierce pace, and was glad he was not in the batsman's shoes.

A short time later, the big man turned to Donald, and said:

"Hi, I'm Tom. Glad to make your acquaintance, sir."

"Hi, I'm Donald. Pleased to meet you too. But what, may I ask, is a yank doing in a place like this?"

"I guess you're right, it is a bit funny. Baseball is my game. I'm a Yankees man, born and bred. My wife wanted to take in the shops in Oxford Street with a few friends. Shop till she drops. So I ducked in here for a few hours. Tell the truth, I've always wanted to know what people mean, when they said to me in the states" It's not *cricket*". So I reckoned this was the best way to find out. Say, you don't exactly sound like you come from these here parts, either." He said with a smile crossing his face.

Before Donald could reply, the tall, thin man leaned over, a flask in his outstretched hand;

"Care for a drink old chaps? Captain McClintock at your service. With Monty in North Africa. *Al Alamein and Tobruk*. Gave old Rommel what for. Damn near bought it though. Tank got a direct hit below me. Got blown clear; I was up top; the other chaps blown to kingdom come. Damn bad show. Still wake up thinking about it."

Tom declined the Captain's offer. Donald felt he should accept just to appear friendly.

"Thanks, Captain, just the job on a day like this." The scotch slid smoothly into his stomach. He got a strong, alcoholic whiff from the Captain's breath.

His thoughts were interrupted by the thunk of leather on willow, followed by a ripple of applause, around the ground.

"Jolly good shot. Well played sir." Said the Captain

"Say, can someone please explain to me the meaning of "*It's not cricket.*"

"Allow me, my good fellow." Replied the Captain. "Cricket was the game of Empire. When Queen Victoria ruled, the game was played in every corner of the Empire. It was a Gentlemen's game. We played by the rules. No cheating. Not in the spirit of the game, old chap. Play up, play the game. People used cricket terms in everyday talk. Like being stumped if they couldn't answer a question. On a sticky wicket if in a spot of bother; like caught in bed with your best friend's wife, having a bit of tallyho. And so on. So if someone was cheating, or behaving badly, we'd say "*It's not cricket*", which was always played honestly, in the correct spirit. Or so everyone thought. Of course later money came into the game; and then the cheating began in earnest. By Jove it did. *The Players*, who came from the lower classes were paid for playing and did anything underhand required to win or get an advantage. *The*

Gentlemen, from the upper class, were even bigger rogues at cheating. And the biggest rogue of all was the great W.G.Grace himself. He pretended to be a Gentleman, and was not paid wages; but he paid himself far more as expenses; and used every low trick in the book, if it helped his cause. Damn bad show."

"Gee, how interesting. Well I never knew. I suppose it goes on now in all professional sports. And business too. It's hard to find honesty these days." Tom replied.

Donald wondered to himself if Maggie Thatcher would be any different if she played cricket. He shook his head. No, not really.

A roar went up from the crowd. Donald turned to see the stumps cartwheeling out of the ground again, following a lightning delivery from the fast bowler at the Pavilion End; and another batsman slowly beginning his long walk back to the dressing room, shaking his head in disbelief.

"Can anyone explain simply to me, what's going on out there? This cricket is sure a funny game. *Groucho Marx* said it was the best cure for insomnia that he knew." Tom asked, eyes twinkling.

This time Donald jumped in first, and answered:

"OK Tom, here's something I just read in the programme, about how to briefly explain cricket to a tourist. It's quite simple, really. Get this:

You have two sides, one out in the field and one in.

Each man that's in the side that's in goes out and when he's out he comes in and the next man goes in until he's out.

When they are all out, the side that's out comes in, and the side that has been in goes out, and tries to get those coming in out.

Sometimes you get a man still in and not out.

When both sides have been in and out, including the not-outs, that's the end of the game.

Alternatively, two men in white coats go out into the middle of the field, and set up two sets of three sticks with smaller pieces of wood balanced on top. When this task is completed, it rains.

"Gee, that's good. I'm now more confused than ever! At least it's not raining." Tom laughed.

"I say old chaps, it looks like that new fellow Botham, coming out to bat for Somerset. Should be worth watching. They say he can hit the ball. Expect he's a future star. Heard that one before." The captain took out a small pair of binoculars, as he spoke.

Donald, saw the young blond colossus striding to the wicket, unhelmeted, swinging his bat in an arc over his head, to loosen up. An expectant hush fell over the crowd. Botham defended the first two balls from the off spin bowler; well flighted and on a length. The third ball was temptingly pitched outside the off stump. Botham stepped down the wicket, his bat flashing like a scimitar, as he flatbatted the ball in the air like an *Exocet* missile towards the offside boundary. Straight towards where they were sitting!

"Quick, hit the deck." Donald roared, and grabbed his two companions by the arm.

As they fell to the ground, the ball smashed into the back of the wooden seat behind them. When Donald stood up the umpire had two hands in the air, signalling a six. The crowd roared approval. There was a slight delay as the ball was replaced.

"Jeepers, I see what you mean about this new guy. He sure can whack 'em. He could do well with the Yankees! Tom said, as he got back on his feet, dusting himself.

"Must be off, chaps. Got to get some more resuscitation at the Tavern bar. Jolly nice to have met you."The Captain said, waving his hand as he limped away, at the end of the over.

"You too, Cap'n. Thanks for explaining about how to play the game in the right spirit. No cheating. I'm going to have fun back in the states, trying to get my friends to follow the rules." Tom shouted after him.

Donald remembered afterwards thinking that the Captain had seemed much more sprightly in his gait as he vanished into the crowd, than when he had first joined them.

On the field, Botham was flaying the bowlers to all corners of the ground. The pigeons gathered at the Nursery End were scattered into the air on numerous occasions as the ball flashed to the boundary. The crowd were in raptures. The sun even got in on the act; as a patch of blue hovered over *Lord's*. Donald felt there was no other place on earth he would rather be.

Tom stood up, a short time later.

"Guess I gotta go. It's just four o'clock. Helluva game. Sure been fun meeting ya." He held out his hand. As Donald shook his hand, an anxious look came on Tom's face.

"Hey, my wallet's gone. Must have dropped out that time we had to duck."

They both scrambled around on hands and knees beneath the wooden seats. To no avail. They looked each other in the eye.

"You thinkin' what I'm thinkin'?" Tom asked, eyebrows raised.

"The Captain? Surely not?"

"Surely yeh. That time we dived, he was the last to get up. And he left pretty soon after."

"You're right, and he seemed to walk a lot faster."

"It's just ain't cricket, is it? Lucky my wife took all my cards for shopping. There was about 300 bucks in it, though." Tom had a rueful smile on his face.

"Yes, it's just not bloody cricket!" Donald agreed.

Tom reached into his overcoat pocket, and said with a sheepish grin on his face

" Hey, I wasn't going to mention it, but I suppose this ain't cricket either." He said as showed Donald the pock-marked cricket ball. It was the *match* ball.

"Picked it up under the seat when we ducked under, thought it would be a nice souvenir. Looks like *God* was punishing me for not playing the game. I don't feel guilty now. I reckon I've paid for it."

"Yes, but it's still not cricket." Donald said with a smile, and sat down to continue watching the game.

A Roman Picture

It wasn't the ideal start to what was supposed to be a relaxing holiday, after working non stop for eight years in one of Dublin's toughest parishes. Father Joe Kane blessed himself as he saw the mask dangling in front of his face, and the French coastline looming large through the airplane window. In spite of hearing the instructions a thousand times, he still needed help to affix the mask properly to his face. Emergency landing in Paris. Ambulances on the runway. Children screaming. People praying out loud. His ears hurting like hell. Medical checkup on his ears, an eight hour delay, before boarding another plane for Rome. Rumour had it the problem was a failure in the air ventilation system in the plane, with the backup system also failing..

Leonardo da Vinci airport was an oven. Rome was baking in an unseasonal heat wave, and was thronged for the upcoming holiday, the feast of the *Immaculate Conception*. Drops of perspiration beaded down the back of his neck.

He checked into his house. Two bedrooms with a view onto the *Tiber*. Looking out the front window across the wide river, St Peter's dome crowned the horizon. Two hundred year old beams across the ceiling of his room. *Perfecto*. One room would be his painting studio. He placed his breviary on the table, and said a silent prayer, thanking God for giving him this holiday.

Next day, Sunday, he rose early, strolled to his local church, and said eight o'clock mass. The sky was blue and cloudless. He walked towards St Peter's square to hear the Pope's ten o'clock mass. Walking through the ancient, cobbled streets, he absorbed the smells, and sounds of the *Eternal City*, and felt he *belonged* there. The rising sun sent slanting shadows across the piazzas, and swallows were swooping and soaring all around. He was dazzled by the artistic perfection of everything. Around almost every corner, a new architectural gem appeared. There was no one in the world he envied, as he crossed the bridge spanning the *Tiber*, and headed for the piazza of St Peter. He recalled the Pope's visit to Ireland, as he beheld the now ageing, trembling Pontiff's open- air mass in the huge square, and afterwards him touring the large crowd in his Pope mobile.

   Returning from the Vatican, he walked along by the river and looked over the wall. A swan was arrowing its way along the water towards the arched eyes of the aged bridge .Elegant neck erect. A ray of sunshine cut through the leafless trees and hit the water where he was gazing. A sudden breeze rippled the water and swayed the rushes at the edges. He felt the urge to paint that scene on canvas.

   After three days of relaxing, and visiting churches and museums in the area, he immersed himself in his painting. He decided to visit the Sistine Chapel the next day, to draw some inspiration from *Michaelangelo's* masterpiece.

   The day came hot and sticky, and he found viewing the magnificent murals and frescoes tiring. In one of the many galleries inside the Chapel, he noticed a tall woman sitting alone, staring up at a painting. She was wearing jeans and sandals, a long-sleeved white blouse and blue cardigan. She had a long neck, and her curling fair hair was tied back behind her head. She was writing in a book on her knee. From a distance he found her strangely alluring, and after three days alone in Rome, felt the urge to communicate with someone. He sat down beside her. She continued writing. He gazed up at the painting. He saw it was the famous *Madonna and Child*, by *Fra Angelico*. One of his favourites. He decided to break the ice.

"It's a wonderful picture. A masterpiece. What do you think? "

"Yes, I agree, I've come back to view it several times."

As she turned to face him, he was startled by her beauty. Behind her silver rimmed glasses, her steel blue eyes seemed to look right into his soul. A serene smile on her oval face. No makeup, or rings on her fingers. He was amazed by her similarity to the *Madonna* in the painting. He guessed she must be about thirty years old, and he also detected an Irish accent.

"What part of Ireland are you from, *Bella Donna*?"

"I'm from Cork. It's my first time in Rome. I've been here two days."

"Really? And what do you *do* back home?"

"I'm a teacher in Liverpool at present. Art is one of my subjects. I'm doing a project on *Renaissance Art*. I hope someday to write a book on it. And you, what brings *you* to Rome?"

"I'm just here to find out what the Romans *do*. My name is Joe Kane. I'm a Social Worker in Dublin. Seriously, I'm here just for a holiday, and inspiration to improve my painting. It's my hobby."

He eventually gleaned her name was Mary Clarke. He couldn't believe how easily he had lied to her. *May God forgive me? He was quite knocked out by her beauty. He would sort it out later, at the right time. He had started, so he had to keep going.*

"There's an open air concert in the *Piazza Navona* tonight. At eight. *Vivaldi's Four Seasons.* Maybe we could meet there at seven and have something to eat beforehand?"

"We've only just met; you might be a serial killer."

"You'll have to take that chance. What do you say?"

"Well ok. I would like that. Here's my hotel number and address."

"I'll collect you then at your hotel. *Ciao* Mary."

"*Ciao* Joe." Their eyes met.

They parted, and he wondered later if he had just dreamt what had happened. He saw that her address was in the area where he was staying. *Probably fictitious. A polite brush off. She would be well used to getting rid of annoying, predatory males. With her looks.*

He was surprised and pleased when she appeared promptly in the foyer of the small hotel. She wore a red, flowery dress and a white ribbon in her hair. Understated, but quite stunning.

"You look lovely Mary, and your perfume is heavenly! What's it called?"

"Flattery will get you everywhere, *Casanova*. Thank you, it's called Temptation."

Oh God, lead me not into temptation. They walked down the cobbled streets.

The *Piazza Navona* was an idyllic background for the concert, with its fabulous fountains, ancient buildings, and bustling nightlife. The music was perfect for the setting. Over the square a sickle moon hung, and stars were scattered in the night sky. The time passed quickly. She was impressed with his command of the Italian language, and his knowledge of Rome. So when he later asked her later if he could take her around the ancient sites the next day, she readily agreed.

"And thanks for tonight. I really enjoyed it. *Ciao*."

"Me too, Mary. *Ciao. A domani.*"

Walking back home he felt elated. He couldn't remember a more enjoyable night .He wondered if she felt the same. But he also felt guilty, because of the deception. *I will come clean, but not at the moment .God please forgive me.*

The following day they toured the old churches in the area, and inside saw many famous paintings of the *Renaissance* period. Mary was busy writing down notes, while he studied the brush strokes and techniques. They sometimes said a short prayer in the churches. Joe had brought his prayer book with him. One time he left it behind him, but she saw it and returned it to him.

"Thanks Mary, I'd hate to have lost it. I've had it a long time."

That night at dinner, Mary wore a white, sleeveless dress with a low neckline, and around her neck a silver chain. She had let her blond hair down, and it reached over her shoulders. She looked quite beautiful. He couldn't take his eyes off her. Neither could the Italian waiters. They got to know each other better.

"Mary, how come someone as beautiful as you isn't married? You must be plagued with guys chasing you." She hesitated, looked down, and finally said.

"Well, I *was* engaged once to someone I dearly loved. We were both very young. Six months before we were to be married, he was killed in a road accident in Cork. I've had lots of friends since, but have never felt the same about anyone. You're the first person I've told this to, in a long time. I still find it hard to talk about it, even after all the years."

"I understand. Sorry to bring up the memory again. I 'm glad you told me. "

After that conversation the night fizzled out, but they agreed to continue touring together the next day. The day was fine and sunny, so they walked to the *Coliseum* and the *Circus Maximus*. He read in a guide book that the Romans came to the *Circus Maximus* not just to watch the careening chariots racing pell-mell around the track. It was the social scene every week, and lots of affairs happened there. On the way home, he decided to put a proposition to Mary at dinner that night. One that had been on his mind for a while.

He was filled with a nerve-tingling excitement, in anticipation of the night ahead. When they settled into an open air restaurant, near the *Pantheon*, he ordered a bottle of *Barolo*, his favourite wine, to impress her. After the wine and the exotic food, and the romantic, moonlight setting, he felt very relaxed. He decided to ask the question bedevilling his mind.

"Mary, I'd like to ask you something rather personal. I would love to use you as a model for a painting I have in mind."

"What kind of painting would that be?" Her eyelashes arched.

"It's a study of the *Madonna*, praying. You'd be perfect. Will you do it?"

"Yes…..yes, I *would* like that." After a minute's hesitation.

The next day was the feast of the feast of the *Immaculate Conception*. Mary arrived at mid-day. The sun was beating down on the cobblestones, and the birds seeking refuge in the cool spray of the fountains.

Mary sat on the bed, with a blue veil covering part of her head and shoulders. He had been trying to capture a certain smile on his canvas, but felt she was a little tense. A break might help. The atmosphere was warm and heavy, with sunlight streaming through the open window. He left the room, and brought back two glasses of red wine, and sat beside her on the bed. The wine went down so smoothly he refilled the glasses. He could get the powerful smell of her perfume. He had never felt so close to her. Her neck lay before him and he instinctively kissed her there. She turned around, and her blue eyes punctured his heart as her lips found his.

When he awoke, he saw Mary returning from the bathroom. She looked as if she had been crying. There were some red marks on the bed clothes.

"Mary, are you alright darling? It's all my fault. I didn't realise. I'm so sorry."

"Nonsense. I'm fine. Why should you ever be sorry for loving someone? It's my birthday by the way, so let's get on and enjoy ourselves, and not feel guilty about it. "

The next morning he hung up the sign *English Spoken* and entered the confessional. It was a quiet morning, but after an hour someone entered and he slowly slid back the grille. He was shocked to smell *that* perfume again. A woman's voice he immediately recognised confessed to having an affair with a man to whom she was not married. He asked her in a low mumbled voice if the man was married, and if she loved him. She hesitated, and said he was not married, and she did not know if she loved him. He pardoned her, and slid back the grille.

The sun dazzled his eyes, as he staggered back to his house. He was shaking. Once more he had deceived and lied to her, and he felt ashamed. And confused. He walked past a church with a large banner draped on it, displaying the words God is Love. *God is Love. Does that mean Love is God? If so then love is everything, and nothing you do to someone in the name of love is wrong, if you truly love that person. Do you love God? Yes he did. Then how could he love another?* He still had a lot of unanswered questions.

There was a letter from Mary in the hall when he returned. She was leaving that night with her art appreciation group for Liverpool. She said how enjoyable he had made her stay in Rome, and hoped they would stay in touch, and signed off the letter "Love Mary". He wondered. In a month's time will she remember? Or will I? He continued to work on his painting over the next few days, and was pleased when he got that facial expression just right. *Perfecto*. He would call it Madonna *Praying*.

Every day since returning to Dublin, memories of his trip to Rome kept flashing into his head. Instead of forgetting Mary, she came into his thoughts more than ever. He realised he was in love with her and wanted to be with her again. *Crazy. I'm a Priest, married to God. She'd be furious to discover my many deceptions. I'm much older, and she may not feel the same about me anyway. I want to marry her, but its madness. I'm married to God. Yes, but with my soul. I will be married to Mary with all my heart. Even Jesus had the company of Mary Magdalene.* He decided then he must visit Liverpool and confront the matter.

It was a drizzly grey morning when he called into St Catherine's School in the suburbs of Liverpool.

"I've come to see Mary Clarke. She's a teacher here."

"Sorry Sir. We don't have anyone here of that name."

"Are you sure? She's from Cork .Blond hair. About thirty years old."

"That sounds like Sister Concepta Mary. She's at prayer. Can you wait Sir, in the waiting room?" *Sister Concepta? It couldn't be her. It must have been a made-up story.*

Joe was dressed in ordinary clothes, and was startled to see Mary enter the room in a grey habit with her blond hair covered by a grey headscarf. She looked pale and unwell.

"Well, this *is* a surprise. I hadn't heard from you. As you can see I owe you an explanation."

"Mary, I am so happy to see you. I'm the one who owes the explanations. I have to confess that I'm a priest, and I've been less than honest with you."

"That's ok, as you can see I haven't been exactly dead straight with you. Anyway, I discovered you were a priest the day you left your missal in the church. A leaflet fell out. I couldn't help reading it. It was about your ordination."

"Then why did you agree to model for me?"

"Well…..because I really liked you and trusted you in spite of the cover-up. And because of the great painter *Fra Angelico.* He was an abbot in the *Renaissance* period, and his model was a nun .They fell in love. She is the lady in the *Madonna and Child* painting. It caused a big scandal then. So it had happened before. Love has no borderlines."

"Mary, does that mean you love me?"

"Yes."

"And I love you Mary, and I want to marry you. But I *can't*."

She looked at him anxiously. Blue eyes flashing.

"Joe, there's something I've got to tell you. I'm *pregnant*. I don't know what to do. I'll have to leave the Order. It's very frightening. I haven't said anything yet to the abbess, or my family."

"But you must tell them both as soon as possible."

"They'll want to have the baby adopted."

"I'll look after you Mary."

"I don't want charity, I need more than that." She snapped.

His head was spinning. He was hit hard by the news, but somehow felt it was all pre-ordained from above. He walked around the room several times, gathering his thoughts and recollecting the plans he had made before coming. After a short while, he replied.

"It's wonderful news Mary, about the baby. And it makes what I'm going to suggest an even better idea. I've just been granted a two year transfer, on medical grounds, to a parish in Rome. I'll have my own house there. *And* I can bring my own housekeeper. It may not be the way we both would like to do it, but we'd be together. *And* in Rome. I *know* we'd be happy there. Will you come and live with me in Rome?"

Mary then paced around the room, head down, hands joined, before she replied

"Yes Joe, I will. I…..I don't think the abbess or my family will be happy. But I think God *would* approve."

He reached over and took her hands in his.

"Great. Let's now go into the oratory and pray for *His* blessing."

"Yes, let's do that. I feel happier already."

A Convenient Arrangement

The June morning sun was glinting on a blue, still sea. On the stony beach, she saw a young boy skimming stones across the water. One. two.. three… four…. Her father had told her long ago that if she could skim a stone seven times, she could achieve anything she wanted in life. She had no interest in these games, they were for boys. Maybe her father wished that she was a boy. She *was* an only child. Well, maybe….

Looking out to sea she saw the *Kish* Lighthouse like a beached spaceship on the horizon, and remembered growing up in Dun Laoghaire, and seeing the old Kish Lightship berthed in the harbour. Then she saw the mail boat pass Howth head on its way to Holyhead. Maybe full of emigrants searching for a better life? Like her? Got to keep thinking positive.

She continued walking along the promenade away from Bray Head, and breathed in the salty air and felt good. She felt the worry about the petty cash recede in her mind. Overhead seagulls wheeled and screeched in the cloudless sky, and some plunged into the sea like winged dive bombers. After passing the Amusements Park, she saw the red bricked Victorian houses, and thought how typically English Bray looked. A miniature Blackpool. She had heard that in the fifties English people flocked to Bray for their holidays. The troubles in the North had put a stop to all that. Now all the hotels were being converted to Nursing Homes. Don't want to end up in one of those…. She shivered at the thought, realising deep down that if it ever happened, she would probably have no say in the matter.

Ahead, across the bay, Killiney Hill loomed, with Dalkey Island jutting out from the shoreline. She felt that on a day like today there must be a real resemblance to the Bay of Naples, although she had never been there. Maybe someday she would go there…. That would make Dalkey like *Sorrento*; and Bray like *Naples*. And the Sugar Loaf *Vesuvius*. Well, maybe…..

Tess Nolan liked to do two lengths of the prom each week, before her Saturday morning coffee in *Lacy's* Hotel with her friend Lily Doyle. They had met a few months earlier at a dancing school in Bray; and discovered they had something in common. They were both thirty something, unmarried, alone, and each with a teenage son to rear.

She quickened her stride as she thought back to her first year at University. Her mother had made her study Commerce. She found it boring, but she was good with numbers. Then she met Johnny, and studying just didn't seem that important anymore. He was in second year Marketing. His blond curls and blue eyes were on her mind night and day. She would never forget his words the night she told him she was pregnant.

"Tess, it must be a mistake. Are you sure? Maybe you should have a second opinion. *You* told me it was safe." He said, pacing the floor in an agitated manner.

"I think you should leave now, Johnny." She was cut to the quick by his words. That was the last time she spoke to him.

Her parents were not sympathetic. Her mother was more worried about the neighbours' reaction than about her or the baby. She was sent on the mail boat to a backstreet doctor in Liverpool. But she decided, at the door of the doctor's house, not to go through with it; and ran away to a local hostel. The Sisters of Charity were her salvation. I *do* owe them, she thought. The sisters looked after her until her baby came; a boy with blue eyes and blond hair. She called him Sean. She recalled how tough those first years were. No support. Her parents and Johnny were history. They were selfish and unloving, she thought bitterly. It was *survival*, plain and simple. She remembered even having to go on the game to make ends meet.

   Sean was five years when she returned to Ireland. Times were tough, but she got a job in the office of a large car dealer in Bray. Pretty soon she was made Office Manager. Her facility with numbers finally proved useful.

   As she sucked in a deep salted breath, she saw the Amusement Park looming up, and the kids queuing up for candy floss, and toffee apples. Beside the park was the Kylemore Nursing Home, where her mother now lived. She had decided last year to break the ice and contact her parents. The new owners of the house in Dun Laoghaire told her that her parents had split up years ago, and her mother had suffered a breakdown and was in a Nursing Home. She had anxiously searched until she tracked her down on the Bray seafront.

   "Mother, it's me Tess. Don't you remember me?"

   "No, I can't remember names any more. It's hard to remember. They put me in here with all these loonies. It's a home for the bewildered, the living dead. I have to go home; it's driving me mad being in a place likes this. Nobody ever visits. And I can't write anymore. Will you get my bags, I want to go home." She started to rise up out of the chair.

"Mam, where's dad, does he visit you?"

"No, I can't say if he does or not. It's lonely here. I want to go home for Christmas. Where's my bag?"

Walking home that day to her rented house in the centre of Bray, she wondered if her running away had contributed to her mother's mental problems. Well maybe, but it's too late for all that now. Got to move on. She had her own problems. Raising a child in Ireland on your own, for god's sake! And the high taxes. And everyone leaving. Still, she thought, I'd hate to end up in a place like that! The very thought of it made her shudder.

She sat at the usual table in the hotel, and waited for Lily, who arrived half an hour late. As normal. But Tess didn't mind. They understood each other, although from different backgrounds, and they had fun together. Lily was an extrovert buxom redhead from Wicklow, and Tess felt she could confide all her innermost thoughts in her. Well, almost all her thoughts. The waiter arrived on cue with their coffees.

"Jeez Tess, sorry I'm late. Couldn't pass those one – armed bandits at the Arcade, without having a blast. Sorry I did now. Pocket money's all gone."

Lily sat down, her breath wheezing in her throat, and lit a fag.

"Have one Tess?"

"No thanks, I'm trying to give them up. You know I'm on a new fitness kick. I'm working up to a sea walk to Greystones next month. Christ, what's wrong with you Lily, you look ghastly!"

"Ah, stop worrying will you, you're a great worrier. It's nothing. It's that time. Either that or I'm preggers. Wouldn't that just beat the band?" She replied smiling.

"How's Mick keeping?" The new boyfriend. They had met a few months earlier at a dance in the Arcadia ballroom. He was a wild looking six foot redhead, with a scraggly red beard.

"Sure he's grand. He moved in with me a few weeks ago. Liam loves him, and they play hurling on the green." Lily said, sipping her coffee.

"What does he do?" Strange she never mentioned them living together, before now.

"He's in the land reclaiming business. He's away a lot. Days on end. I don't pry. It's his affair."

"Wasn't that terrible Lily, about the Miami Showband up north? The friggin' murderers! And poor Fran O'Toole. One of our own. All so young. Are you going to the funeral?"

"I'm gutted. Sure weren't they playing at the dance in the *Arcadia*, when me'n Mick met? Yeh, I'll be there."

"Lily, I'm worried about my job at the garage. I've heard a rumour Paul Murphy is selling out. After more than twenty years. The site is worth a fortune. What will I do? I've earned good money there for over five years."

"There you go worrying again. Might never happen. Sure you're great anyways with the numbers. You'll get something. Mind you, you've done *ok*, with Sean going to Pres. Bray, and having a grand little house on the Meath Road."

"Hear the Royal Showband are coming to the *Arcadia* next month? Fancy going?" Tess changed the subject.

"Great. I love going to the Ark. Have to get rid of this dose first. Might go to see Ernie Piggott as well in the *Sunnybank* one of these nights. They say he's a great one with the ladies, and he's a great singer too."

Walking up Putland Road later, to Pres Bray to collect Sean, Tess's mind was racing. There were some things you couldn't tell, even to your closest friend. Last night she had met Paul Murphy as normal for Friday night dinner at eight in the *Esplanade Hotel.* After their usual champagne meal, they adjourned to a room upstairs. Later, lighting one of his favourite Cuban cigars, he had nonchalantly announced

"Tess, I've got something to tell you. Good news and bad news. I've decided to sell the business and retire. My accountant tells me it's a good time to go, and I've got a good offer. In fact one I couldn't refuse. Better than the figures show; in fact the last five years our margins have been quite poor." He lifted the brandy glass to his lips, and stared hard into her eyes.

She stared back. He *knew*. Probably suspected all along. But knew she'd blow the lid on their five year affair to his wife and four children, if he confronted her. Anyway there's a price for everything. Paul, the great car salesman knew that more than anyone. She had a son to rear, after all.

"Lucky for you I know where all the bodies are buried, Paul. And the bad news?"

"It's the end for us Tess, I'm afraid. You know I love you, but you know what they say about blood and water. I've just bought a 40 ft yacht; and I'm going on a month's trip to the West Indies with Maureen and the kids. I'm sorry." He reached out for her hand.

She recoiled from his reach. She knew they had been using each other. A convenient arrangement. Panic began to set in at the thought of the sudden change in her life just sprung on her; but even though she knew deep down that she didn't love him, there was a comfort factor in being with Paul.

"I suppose you know best, Paul. Goodbye." She replied as she put on her coat and grabbed her handbag and headed for the door.

"Tess, we can still be friends. Hey, don't say goodbye like that. That's not the way to leave. What about the past five years?" he pleaded.

"What about them? You go your own bloody way, and I'll go mine. You go to your family and I'll go to bloody mine. I guess it's a blood and water thing. Goodbye Paul."

She slammed the door behind her, and walked down the stairs, dabbing her eyes as she went. Goddamit, why cry if you don't love him? She couldn't understand why she felt so dejected. She had probably said goodbye to her job too. But she wasn't going to beg. Anyway the new owner probably had his own plans for the office. Then the thought of next week's due diligence audit by the new owner hit her. And would she be able to cover up the fact of the money siphoned out of the petty cash over the time with Paul? As she walked home alone along the dimly lit streets, a cold wind blew up behind her from the sea, and a light rain began to fall. She covered her head, and quickened her steps past the *Carlisle* grounds, over the Quinsboro' Road, and back to Meath Road. She felt a loneliness that she had not felt for a long time. A feeling of rejection, and despair about the future. Like a train going into a never-ending tunnel of darkness.

Lily cancelled their meeting the next week, saying she felt unwell. Poor Lily, she has her problems too. Paul was very cool to her in the office all week. But the audit never happened. Probably deferred until the new boss arrived, so *he* could do the dirty work. On the last Friday before the company sale, Paul met her in the corridor and said curtly:

"Oh Tess, by the way the new owner said for you to come in on Monday. He'll
talk to you then about the future. The other office staff have been let go. Goodbye."

As he turned to go into his office, he lifted the cigar from his lips, looked deep into her eyes, smiled, and added: "And good luck."The final words. He always had to have the final say. An uneasy knot formed in her stomach.

After her walk next day to feed the swans in the harbour, and back to the hotel to meet Lily, she felt more relaxed. Low scudding clouds on the sea and rain on the wind. She moved fast.

When Lily finally arrived, Tess was startled by her appearance.

"God Lily, you look like the *Wreck of the Hesperus*. What happened you?"

Lilly started sobbing, and wringing the handkerchief in her hands. It was a while before she could speak. Her eyes were raw red.

"I had to go to hospital for tests last week, cos' I was feeling lousy."

"Why didn't you tell me, I would have gone with you? Did Mick bring you?"

"No. Mick wasn't there. Away on business. I'm finished with him. Kicked him out. He's no good to me. Never there when he's needed.

"You're right, Lily. *Men*. Never there when you need them. You unfortunate creature. Having to endure all that on your own…Say, what about the two of us going to the *Sunnybank* next Friday. I'm free this week. How about it? We'll get you dickied up and you'll knock 'em out.Give 'em the old razzle dazzle. Well?" There was a long pause.

"Yes, I think so. Yes, let's do that. That would be fun. Yes, I'd like that"

Lily's face lit up and a sparkle flashed in her eyes, like a meteor in the heavens.

"Miss Nolan, could you drop into my office now please. I need to discuss some things with you."The voice sharp and direct.

Her hand was trembling as she pushed open the door, and walked in. At the same moment he swivelled around in his black leather chair to face her. She gasped. It was the blue eyes, piercing like an arrow even though bespectacled now; and the now greying curls receding from his temples.

"Johnny!" She stood frozen at the door.

"Tess Nolan. It *is* you. I don't believe it. After all these years. Do come in and sit down. I'll order coffee. This…….. is a shock. Quite unexpected."He *did* seem genuinely surprised. But he was always able to put on an act. She saw the wedding ring on his hand.

"Married Johnny? Any family?"

"Yes to the first. For six years. *No* to the second. And you?

"Still looking for the right guy. I'm very fussy."

"So Paul told me. He spoke highly of you. Said you were a genius with figures. And if I might say so your own figure is in remarkably good shape."

"I work on it. What else did he tell you?" The coffee arrived just then.

"Black as usual?" he asked, smiling as he poured. She nodded, and felt her eyes magnetised to his, and thought they had the aquamarine hue of the sea in them. He handed her the cup, and she quickly diverted her gaze.

"Nothing much else. The figures speak for themselves. I was going to have an in-depth audit of the office done by my staff. But I think we can work out a new program out between us. I want to take this company *onwards* and *upwards*. You're a key player in my plans, Tess. Are you with me?" She knew he had re-written the script as she replied:

"Sure Johnny, I'm with you."

"Thanks. Say, I'd like to take you to dinner on Friday night if you're free. We have a lot of planning to do."

"Sorry. I have a date. Also your wife might not approve." You're pushing your luck Johnny, she thought. Fool me once.

"Of course. I should have expected an attractive lady like you to have had a date most Fridays. Maybe some other time then. My wife likes to play poker every Friday. I like to work. We do our own thing."

Walking home that evening, her thoughts raced. Why did she not mention Sean? It just wasn't the right time, she realised. But she felt a slight thrill in the way things had panned out. What shocked her was the realisation that although she hated him bitterly for the past, she had never once met anyone since that excited her as much.

It was late on Friday, a week later; Johnny summoned her to his office.

"Hi Tess, exciting news, our Italian car suppliers are launching a new range of cars for the Irish market next year. There's a five day conference for all major dealers to kick start the launch in *Sorrento* next month. I'd like you to come as part of the team. I need a financial input. Will you be free to travel?"

"That's really exciting, Johnny. It's just my mother is very ill at the moment. I'll have to think about it."

On the Saturday morning Sean accompanied her on her walk down the prom. The morning sun was glittering on the diamond sea, and a few fleecy clouds hung in the sky like abandoned sheep. Sean ran down onto the stony strand, blond curls streeling in the wind.

"Hey Ma, watch me bowling." He had just joined the Bray cricket team. He picked up a few rounded pebbles, and started to bowl them into the sea. The disturbed seagulls rose shrieking in fury from the waves. He then picked up a flat stone and skimmed it into the water. One. Two..three…four….five…..six……seven…….

"Hey Ma, did you see that?"

"Yes I did, well done son!" she clapped her hands, and something registered deep down inside her.

She felt as if she had thrown the stone herself, and a feeling of elation swept over her body. She felt for the first time the confidence that she could succeed in anything she wanted. A feeling of relief swept over her. The empty pang in her stomach was gone.

The thought of *Sorrento* then hit her as she saw the mail boat gently moving east past the *Kishbank*. She had decided not to get involved again with any man after her experience with Paul. But as she looked up the coastline to Dalkey Island, she wondered what the *Isle of Capri* would be like. And *Pompeii*. And *Naples*. And mandolin music sweet in the breeze, on the balcony of a hotel overlooking an azure sea. And… well maybe.

Day and Night

Johnny Cassidy had two big heroes in his life. The first was his father, who had fought with the IRA in the war of Independence, against the *Black and Tans*. There was a picture on the wall at home in Dundalk of a man in uniform, below the picture of the Sacred Heart. Johnny was in his teens when he found out the soldier's name was Michael Collins.

"Dad, did you know the *Big Fella?*"

"No. Not really. *Nobody* did. He liked it that way. I met him once though. He shook my hand. I'll always remember that." His father's eyes seemed misty and faraway then.

"It must have been exciting in those days."

"No, Johnny. Anything but. They were bad times." He sensed his father didn't want to talk anymore.

He loved hunting with his father in the *Mournes*. His father was an expert wing shot, and he soon developed his own skill with the gun. It was during the hunger strikes in the early eighties, that he and his older brother Mick joined the Provos.

His second big hero was Frank Sinatra. He not only shared Sinatra's blue eyes, but had a fine voice too. He learned all Sinatra's songs. He soon became the crooner with a local band.

The pain slammed through his skull in short sharp darts, like arrows raining down on his brain. His legs felt on fire when he tried to move. Through his half open eyelids, he saw above him a hazy circle of green masked faces, encircling a blinding light. Sleep was pulling him down, as words floated like clouds through his head.

"Lucky to be alive. Severe concussion. Brain seems ok. May have initial amnesia episodes, but memory should recover in time. One broken leg. And second degree burns on both legs. Plenty of stitching. No major surgery required."

"Yes, the car was completely burnt out. He just got out in time. That poor guard wasn't so lucky. *He's* on a life support machine. "

"We need 24 hour observation for the first week. Then it will be plenty of R&R, before the Gardai take over. I suspect they will be looking to enforce a further period of rest -- at the state's expense of course!"

What was going on? What had happened, and why was he lying here?

As he drifted into unconsciousness, his mind filled with hazy thoughts.

.

There was a girl who had quite bewitched him. Maggie Connolly. She came from a large family in Ardee with strong republican sympathies. Blazing red hair, green eyes, and a tall, shapely body. He was in his late twenties when they met, at one of his gigs. She was nineteen. Her family didn't approve. The relationship was only six months old, when his world turned upside down.

He was involved in a botched bank robbery in the North. It was a set up.

The police, armed and waiting, caught them unawares. He drove the getaway car. Of the three who went into the bank, two died, and one was captured. A security man was also killed. He alone escaped over the border.

The next day he was summoned to a meeting by his commanding officer.

"Johnny, its bad news, not only did we lose two good men yesterday, but the injured one *sang*. Like a canary. They're after you. You'll have to leave the country. Immediately."

"Are you sure, you might be mistaken?"

"No. I'm positive. We have our sources."

"Well, for how long and where?"

"Indefinitely. We'll contact you when it's safe. We have arranged all you need. *Marbella.* Not the worst place in the world. Just remember to lie low and keep your mouth shut. We have ways of dealing with traitors, as your injured colleague will soon find out."

His six years on the *Costa del Sol* had passed peacefully. He got a singing job with a local group doing the expatriate cabaret circuit. He often thought of Maggie, and how he hadn't contacted her before he left. But everything had happened so quickly. Anyway how could he explain everything to her? *And* her family. Anyway she was so young. She would probably start a new life with someone else. And maybe he would be able to return sometime. He had many new relationships, but she was always at the back of his mind. He always finished his cabaret act singing *One for my Baby (and one more for the road)*. In his mind this was *their* song.

He liked the Spanish sunshine in the winter months. But he missed the buzz and excitement of home. And the *craic*. In fact he sometimes found the *Costa* lifestyle artificial and boring. His mother's death had hit him like a hammer. *And* the guilt at not being able to attend her funeral.

The sun was a blazing ball in a duck blue sky. Johnny placed his half empty glass of *sangria* on the table beside the swimming pool, and lay back on his sun chair in the shade, book in hand. The snow clad *Sierras* split the skyline. A humming bird hovered over the purple bougainvilleas in the garden. Below, the waves washed onto the dark sand of the packed beach. The telephone ring cracked the silence. It was his eldest brother Mick.

"Johnny can't talk too long. I'd like to see you urgently. I'm flying to *Malaga* today, and returning later in the night. Can you meet me at three at the *Alay* Hotel?"

"Sure, Mick. See you there."

As he replaced the receiver, a dry feeling welled up inside his mouth. He felt his past about to catch up again on him.

After a period of chat about life back home, Mick cut to the chase.

"Johnny, some of your old colleagues in arms want to do one final bank heist, just over the Border. They want *you* in. You're a safe pair of hands, and have the experience. There's a million in it for you. What do you say?"

Johnny hesitated, sipped his martini, and replied.

"No. Thanks for the offer, Mick, but no thanks. I'm out of that scene now. And what about the *Peace Process*, for Christ's sake? What would the big chiefs say?"

"Apparently nothing. They'll turn a blind eye to it. They'll get their cut too, of course. It suits their strategic planning. Will you re-consider?"

"No, That's it. Final."

"There's one other thing, Johnny. Dad took a stroke last week. He's in a wheelchair and can barely speak. They give him three months at most. He told me his dearest wish is to see you again before he dies."

He realised then he had no choice. *And* the money would be useful.

"Ok, count me in. You always had a way of getting what you wanted."

Johnny glanced nervously at his watch. *Should never have agreed to do this. Bad feeling in my gut.* Two forty. The Doran brothers, Francie and James were now in the bank five minutes. He had checked all the streets in the area beforehand. There were two escape routes. But he also noticed a narrow one way street beside the bank, which he would risk in a complete emergency. *Damn*, what's keeping them? He suddenly got that nervous feeling he had in the previous botched raid. They had to be over a railway crossing ten minutes drive away by three o'clock as a long goods train would pass through then. He decided to play his hunch, and drove his stolen van out of the car park, across the street and stopped outside the bank. Just then an alarm sounded, followed by several gunshots , and the two men burst out onto the street , one holding a black bag and pistol , the other a sawn off shotgun. They bundled into the van, swearing viciously

"I fuckin' told you Francie, no shooting."

"That fuckin' guard, he set off the alarm. He had it comin'."

Johnny put his foot to the floor, and veered wrong way up the laneway, as squad cars, sirens blaring and lights flashing blockaded the other escape routes. At two minutes to three they crossed the level crossing and headed for the forest where the other escape car was hidden. The long goods train gave them the head start they needed.

They crossed the back roads over the border and stopped to bury the money, as planned, in a remote wooded area. Afterwards they drove towards the main Dublin road. They began to feel quite elated about pulling it off. Then, rounding a sharp bend, he saw a Garda car blocking the road, with an unarmed Garda standing in front of it. *Shit* .He accelerated towards the

Garda car, and smashed off the side into a nearby tree. He vaguely remembered the Dorans telling him to run for it as he crawled out, and the petrol fumes everywhere as the car burst into flames.

When he woke again in the hospital he had been moved to a private room. He blinked as the sunlight streamed through the window. His bandaged head no longer ached. A shadowy figure hovered at the end of his bed. It was his brother Mick.

"Johnny, how are ye old son. You look a sight."

"Fine, Mick, fine. I'll be singing again in a few weeks."

"Good man. That kind of singing is ok. I'm here to warn you that if you sing to the cops you're *brown bread*, and so is dad. Your brothers and I are ok. We're still useful to the cause. You understand, don't you, it's *not* my decision?"

"Sure, I understand. Everything will be ok. Don't worry. I can't remember a thing."

"That's good, Johnny. Just make sure it *stays* that way. There's a bottle of whiskey in your locker. For medicinal purposes, of course." He winked.

"Of course." He drifted away again as the dark clouds descended.

He awoke later to see two uniformed Gardai standing at his bedroom door. A tall, lean man, in plain clothes, stood looking down on him.

"Ah, awake at last, Johnny. Inspector Pat Coleman. I was a fan of yours once. Your voice could charm the birds off the trees. And into bed too, if what I heard was true. I must warn you though, whatever you say will be taken down. We have a few questions to ask you about the bank robbery six years ago. *Serious* questions. But today, it's just the matter in hand. We have the murder of a security guard, a major bank robbery, and a critically injured Garda. For starters. You're in trouble, Johnny. *Deep* trouble. Minimum ten to fifteen years. You'll be an old man. A complete sworn confession now, everything you know, your accomplices, where the money is. Then we might get it reduced to half. What do you say?"

"I can't remember anything. I want to see a lawyer."

"We could look favourably on the previous robbery."

"No. I can't remember. *Bring on the Clowns.*"

"What sort of rubbish are you talking? Your head is going or gone. Ok. It's *your* life. A life sentence is a long time. Think about it." Inspector Coleman swept out the door.

W hen he awoke that night the room was dark, save for the pale moonlight streaming through the window. He felt a presence in the room.

"Who's there?"

"It's your night nurse."

She stepped out of the shadows. His heart jumped.

"Maggie. Jesus it's you. I don't believe it. I must be delirious!"

"Yes Johnny, it's me. It *is* quite a coincidence. I heard you were admitted, and managed to swap with another nurse. I needed to talk to you. I didn't want anyone else looking after you."

"And neither do I."

"Don't think that changes anything. I still haven't got over how you left me. The false promises. I was foolish to think I was any different from all the other ladies you loved and left. You broke my heart. Into pieces. *Indeed.* The least you owe me is an explanation!"

As she moved closer to the bed, he saw she was even more beautiful than he remembered. Her red hair hung long over her white uniform. His heart raced.

"Maggie, I'm truly sorry. From the bottom of my heart. I had to get out overnight after the botched Dungannon bank job. No choice. A life on the run was no life for a young, beautiful girl like you. And what about your family? What would they think?"

"You didn't give *me* much choice in the matter, did you?"

"No. I *do* regret that. But you were always on my mind."

"You'd say mass if you knew the words. Now take this medicine, and let me get on with my job."

The next night she told him that she had been in a serious relationship for the past two years. The relationship had recently broken up. He felt that night that her feelings towards him had slightly softened. He resolved to do something the following night to try to break down the wall between them.

Maggie entered the room the next night later than usual, locked the door, walked to the window, and pulled the curtains.

"I've finished my round, so we can relax a few minutes together."

"Great, Maggie. Could you hand me that bottle of whiskey in my locker?"

"Ok. But not for me. I'm on duty."

"I thought you'd finished your round."

"Well yes. But I'm on call for another hour. Maybe later."

Well, not a complete refusal. Encouraging. He knocked back two quick shots of whiskey. He felt his confidence growing.

"Maggie, do you remember that game we used to play, years ago? At special moments."

"Yes Johnny, the *Sinatra* game."

"Maggie, we're just like *Strangers in the Night*. Two lonely people."

"Yes, and you've got me *Bewitched, Bothered, and Bewildered*."

"*Night and Day*, you are the one."

"I think *I've Got You under My Skin*."

"It's just the *Nearness of You*. That thrills and excites me.

"And I do *Get a Kick out Of You*. You know that. So, let's *Begin the Beguine*."

"Maggie, come *Fly with Me*."

"Ok Johnny, *Fly Me to The Moon*."

He suddenly felt her beside him in the bed, whispering in his ear.

"This time we do it *My Way*. You have no choice."

He awoke later to find Maggie, hair ruffled, sitting beside him, holding his hand.

"You're temperature's up."

"I'm not surprised."

"I'll give you a sedative."

"Did I dream what happened?"

"No. Here take this medicine."

"Maggie, I've just realised I can now remember about the robbery. It's like a veil has been lifted."

"Really, everything?"

"Yes, except my colleagues' names, and where we hid the cash."

He recounted everything he could recall about the robbery, before drifting into a deep slumber.

It was about mid day the next day. He was elated at how the night had gone with Maggie. He felt the dark depression clouds were at last lifting from his mind.

The door burst open. Inspector Coleman swung in, followed by a group of Gardai, and marched to his bedside.

"I'm formally charging you with involvement in the Dungannon bank raid six years ago. Thanks to the good work of Ban Garda Connolly here, in taping your admission, you'll get eight to ten years. I will also be charging you with the current raid. I think you should consider again my offer of mitigation. You have one more day to make up your mind."

He was stunned. His stomach knotted with shock. And fear. Maggie stood tight lipped behind the Inspector, her eyes fixed on a spot high on the wall behind him. He had fallen into a trap. Yes, a *Tender Trap*. Lulled into a web of false love and deceit. Yes indeed, *The Lady is a Tramp. How she must have enjoyed giving me a taste of my own medicine. Should have known better. Revenge is a bitter pill*

Later that day Maggie entered Inspector Coleman's office. She sat down in front of his desk, and looked into his steely grey eyes.

"Maggie, I've recommended you for promotion. Congratulations. You did a fine job. I believe you had a fling with him once. *Ol' Blue Eyes*. You showed excellent control in not letting your emotions get in the way of your professional duty. By the way, Sheila and the kids are off to visit her mother next weekend. Would you be free for dinner on Friday night?"

"Maybe, I'll let you know."

As she walked out the door, she wondered if her promotion had something to do with the affair they'd had for the past two years. An affair going nowhere! *Her* achievements wouldn't damage *his* prospects either!

Johnny spent a restless night, racking his head for a way out of the nightmare. In vain. He'd have to *Face the Music and Dance.* Ah well, *That's Life*, he thought. He continued tossing and turning.

The next morning, he was taken in a wheelchair down the corridor for xrays. The male nurse wheeled him into the lift, and pressed the button. He was wheeled out of the hospital into the back of an ambulance. Soon they were speeding down the road, siren blaring.

"What's going on? Where are you taking me?"

"Relax. Back to where you came from, boy. By land and air to sunny Spain. All expenses paid."

"You guys really amaze me. How did you manage it, with the hospital crawling with security?"

"Your brother Mick had a hand in it. But we needed help from the inside. Your night nurse was the key."

"You don't say."

"I do say. She must think a lot of you. She asked me to give this letter to you."

His fingers trembled, as he opened the envelope, and read.

"Dear Johnny,

Don't worry. I erased all the intimate bits from the tape. You should now be heading *South of the Border*. When you've settled back, please call or write. This time. I love you. *All the Way*. Maggie."

Yes, he felt his spirits rising again. Yes, he would call her this time. Yes, he was going to add a new song to his repertoire. One he had avoided over the years. *Love and Marriage*. He smiled, and started humming softly to himself.

Freedom

A bitter wind blew out of a grey November sky, as Sean Bonner walked out of Mountjoy jail, clutching a parcel that contained all his precious possessions. It was Friday mid morning and the early Dublin traffic congestion had given way to midday frustration, with taxis, buses, juggernauts, lorries, and cars fighting it out on the streets before him. A clamped car was being lifted onto the back of a lorry as the angry owner looked on in despair. Sean immediately felt less secure in himself. *Jungle law*, he thought to himself *kill or be killed*.

At Dorset Street he turned right towards O'Connell Street, and a light mist began to fall as the wind blew the dead yellow leaves and rubbish around the street. He pulled up his anorak hood over his shaven head and walked head down into the wind.

Free at last, three long years that felt like three long winters. Good behaviour had shortened his sentence by six months. *It pays to lick arse in Ireland... The screws were ok once you kept your nose clean.* But he had to put up with the merciless taunting of the other inmates because he was a loner, and did not get involved in their ritual games and schemes which mostly involved drugs, alcohol, and sexual perversion.

He had a lean six foot frame under a narrow tight lipped face. He was nicknamed the *Slasher*, because of a knife scar down his right cheek inflicted in a teenage gang fight, and also his conviction for stabbing a young Chinese student outside a late nite disco in Dun

Laoghaire, four years earlier. The student survived, but was crippled for life.

The Judge said he had taken Sean's age and family background into account. Sean was 21 years then, and had been beaten as a child by his drunkard father, who also regularly beat his mother. He was reared in a tough council estate with his three older brothers. His father had died when he was twelve years old, falling from a high, unprotected scaffolding while repairing slates on St Michael's Church, a day after he had been on a binge.

His mother alone reared the family, cleaning houses to supplement her meagre state pension, and his three older brothers had fled to England as quickly as they could to work on the buildings.

Sean and his mother had a close relationship. They lived alone until Sean had fallen for Janey O'Connor, who lived nearby in Monkstown Farm. She was a year older than Sean, and hung out with his gang. Janey was blond, beautiful and vivacious, and Sean was immediately smitten by her. They wanted to marry as soon as possible, and Sean convinced his mother, who had just been diagnosed with Parkinson's disease, to let Janey move into the house. His mother agreed. Reluctantly.

"You'll really like her and she'll help out in the house".

"Whatever you say son, you know best."

Janey was working as a waitress in *Scott's* pub in Dun Laoghaire, and Sean for a plumber in Blackrock named Gerry Allen whom he had met in the pub. Saving to get married was more difficult than either realised, as Janey was an avid shopper, and Sean liked to socialise regularly with his friends. Still they managed to save a reasonable amount after one year. The relationship at home between Janey and his mother was tense at best, and he realised they just about tolerated each other.

Then came the night of the incident. Sean was so drunk at the time he could hardly recollect the scene in Court. He genuinely felt sorry for the victim. Yet he almost felt as if the attack was carried out by a different person.

In prison in the beginning, he liked watching television and looking forward to Janey's frequent visits .These visits became less regular as time went by, and lately had become very infrequent indeed. Of course, he understood she had to take on another job to keep their marriage fund growing, *and* his mother's health was deteriorating rapidly.

She did write regularly and he liked reading her letters over and over. He kept every one in his parcel of belongings, along with photographs of her in the various new dresses she had bought. Mainly for her work, she explained. In her last letter she mentioned that Sean's mother was in a nursing home but would soon return home.

He dreamt a lot of Janey, and getting married, and seeing her beautiful on her wedding day. *And* in bed. A lot in bed. These thoughts helped him to survive when the dark days came and threatened to bring him down into the depths of despair he saw in some of the other inmates. But now he was *free* and returning home, early too, to his one true love. He took out a picture of Janey, in a bikini, and smiled to himself. He couldn't wait. He felt the excitement tingling in his bones.

Walking down *Nth Frederick Street*, past *Findlater's Church*, and along *O'Connell Street*, in the driving rain, he looked into *Clery's* windows, wondering if Janey ever shopped there, as his mother had always done. Looking up at the enormous spire he thought of Janey in bed and smiled again to himself. He could hardly contain himself.

An urchin came up to him.

"Give us the price of the pitchers mister."

"Fuck off and get a job."

"Aw fuck off yerself, yeh bleedin' tosser!"! said the kid running away .

As he walked up to the *Halfpenny Bridge*, he saw the winos lying on the new boardwalk beside the dreary, smelly river Liffey. He crossed over the Halfpenny bridge to return to *Tara Street* station. There was an elderly blind lady, with her white stick, waiting for someone to help her cross the busy road. Nobody did. He took her hand and helped her over. Then there was a gang of drug addicts outside the station wheeling children in a pram. He saw a poster with the newspaper headlines. *Celtic Tiger Economy Boom Rolls On*. He shook his head, ascended the stairs, and bought a ticket to Dun Laoghaire.

Looking out the misted window in the train he could barely see the outline of the harbour as the clouds hung low over a swollen, grey sea.

Janey will be so surprised and delighted to see me home early. I can't wait to see the look on her face. When we're married we'll go to Australia, where the sun always shines, and people live happy lives in the great outdoors. Not like here.

He walked up *Marine* road and stopped into *Scott's* pub for a few shots of hot whiskey to warm himself up. He asked about Janey but no one seemed to know anything about her. *Strange, must be a lot of new staff here.*

At last he reached his mother's rain drenched house where Janey lived. He was surprised to see a dilapidated black Nissan van parked outside. He immediately recognised the banger Gerry Allen, the plumber, always used.

Removing the key from his parcel, he quietly opened the rear door and entered the kitchen. The radio was playing Dean Martin's" *That's Amore* ". On the kitchen table was a large, full ashtray, recently used, and two empty glasses beside a half empty vodka bottle. An opened plumber's toolbox also lay on the table.

He heard a noise upstairs and tiptoed into the hall. He heard Janey's voice " Ohhhhh, Gerry , don't do that ",breaking off into a giggle that he recognised immediately as relating to something very intimate that he himself had long ago experienced with her. He pictured Gerry Allen, with his beard, ponytail, braces, and lumberjack shirt, and medallion around his neck, and the thought made his body shake with rage.

Returning to the kitchen, he looked into the opened toolbox, took out a large metal hammer, walked to the hallway door, hesitated, and then went back into the kitchen and replaced the hammer in the box.

Suddenly, he clearly heard Janey's voice cry out upstairs "Ohhhh Gereeeee"! He walked back to the kitchen table, opened the drawer, took out the large carving knife, walked into the hall, and tip-toed quietly up the stairs.

Goodbye

    Dawn was breaking on the cliffs looking out onto the Baily Lighthouse. The gulls swooped and wheeled, screeching around the rocks, washed by the swell of the waves. High above, the sky gave hope for the day ahead. Staring into the mass of water, he felt hypnotised by the rise and fall of the waves. Up and down, down and up. *How easy it would to be rid of all my worries and pressures in the deep. Dark and inviting. Down, down, down into the dark abyss, and then nothing.*

    Harry Roberts placed the half empty Vodka bottle on the grass beside him; and thought on how, at just thirty three years, he had arrived in this situation.

    His father was a Bank Manager, who liked horse racing. Harry remembered when he was sixteen, his father first brought him to Leopardstown. He was hooked by the whole atmosphere, the style of the dressed -up ladies, the excitement of the crowd, the horses with flaring nostrils and bulging eyes. And the jockeys in their multi - coloured silks. *And* the thrill of the race.

    "What do you think of your first time here, Harry?"

    "Great Dad, and gee you know so many people here, even owners, and trainers!"

    "Yes, some are business acquaintances, others people I've got to know over the years. Here's a few quid. I just got a tip for *Royal Flush* in the next race, and the odds are good at 10 to 1. Why don't you have a flutter?"

His father had omitted to say then, that his business friends usually paid for his expenses at the races, including bets. His father felt it would be bad for business not to accept their hospitality.

Harry was thrilled when *his* horse came romping home; and even more so when he collected his fifty pound winnings. He was so delighted, he hugged his father, who had also backed the same horse.

"Thanks Dad, for bringing me here. This is the best day of my life!"

"You must be my lucky omen Harry, I feel I can't go wrong today!"

From that day on, he went with his father to race meetings as often as he could. He found that by studying the form guide and racing statistics, he often came home making a small gain. He had a head for figures. His father sometimes let him place his bets, and he noticed that his father's smallest bet was never less than 100 pounds; which made him realise what a great job his father had. His dad was the greatest dad in the world!

Harry also noticed that his father was not as successful as *he* was in his betting, but that never deterred him, and he would say with a smile:

"Harry, winning isn't everything, it's the thrill of the chase, and the whole excitement of the day that counts. Whatever the cost, it's worth it! You can't win them all, but it's great fun trying. Anyway, there's always another day!"

One day he overheard his father having a very heated conversation with a tall thin man in a long black coat, carrying a black briefcase.

"For God's sake Jimmy, you know I'll pay you back, I just need a little more time. This is the last time, please, I just need a break. Please don't let me down."

The tall thin man rolled his eyes up to the heavens, scratched his head, looked him in the eyes, and said:

"Paddy, because you're an old friend, and customer, I'm giving you one final chance. Screw up again and there *will* be trouble!"

He reached into the briefcase and handed his father a large brown envelope.

"Thanks Jimmy, you won't regret it."

When his father returned, Harry asked him:

"Who was that funny looking geezer, Dad?"

"Oh, don't mind him, he's a client of the Bank. He often prefers to do business with me here rather than in the Bank. We just pretend to swop roles, for the craic!"

Harry realised then that he was foolish to ever worry about his Dad, who really was the greatest dad in the world!

His Dad was really proud of Harry's academic progress, and told him that the day he attended Harry's conferral was the proudest moment of his life! And he was even happier when Harry landed a top financial job in one of Ireland's largest Banks. Harry soon moved out into an expensive apartment, near the new IFSC building on the Dublin quays, where he worked.

A year later, Harry's father announced that he had retired from the Bank, aged fifty, after 25 years service. Everyone in the family was stunned. Paddy looked a bit shocked himself. He said it was part of a new strategic management restructure in the Bank, and he had been given an offer he couldn't refuse.

"I couldn't afford to turn down the offer. I would have been crazy not to accept it. We've never had so much cash, and now we can all relax, and really enjoy life, and do all the things together that we've never been able to do before."

The whole family then agreed with him that it *was* good news, but Harry kept thinking of the tall thin man, and that conversation with his father at the races.

Six months later, nothing much had changed in their lives, and his father's lump sum seemed to have been quickly depleted, and his mother was still struggling to make ends meet. The household bills continued to flow in, and were not being paid on time. His father was now spending more time at the races, but now having to pay his own expenses. He was also spending more time at night in the local pub.

One night, when visiting, Harry heard his mother and father having a very animated conversation:

"Paddy, I can't cope any more with these unpaid bills, and threatening letters. We haven't had a holiday in years! You've got to do something about it, for God's sake! What happened to all the money you got from the Bank?"

"Well I had some outstanding debts to clear, and the day to day expenses are high. Don't worry darling, I still have plenty, I'll sort everything out, and we'll both go on a holiday to Italy, to *Venice* where we spent our honeymoon. We both need a break from all this pressure!"

His mother relented, but they never got to Italy. His father took a job in a Bookie's shop. It meant he no longer could attend race meetings, but at least he was involved indirectly in the business, and he could still have a "flutter". But his luck was out on the horses, and the financial pressure at home remained. Then, after nine months, his father was dismissed from his job. No reason was given. Harry heard later that it had happened following an internal audit of the shop, by the owners. There were unexplained cash shortages over the months his father had been employed.

His father became very withdrawn, and didn't go out much, except to the pub, and most days he had arguments with Harry's mother, mainly over money. Four months after losing the job, he suffered a mental breakdown, and was hospitalised. Harry remembered a conversation they had during a visit to the hospital:

"Harry, you know the best days were when we were together at the races. The great times we had, even if we didn't always win. Nothing else mattered, once the starter's flag fell! I really miss those days, the thrill and excitement of it all, and I think a lot about them, and it's killing me that we can't do it now."

"Yes Dad, it's the same for me too. But we'll do it again. Don't forget, there's always another day!"

His father died six months later. They say he just lost the will to live. At the burial in Sutton graveyard on a bleak January morning, with a biting wind blowing in from the sea, he was surprised to meet an unexpected mourner at the graveside. It was the tall thin man, still dressed in a long black coat.

"Your old man was a good guy, kid. A gentleman. Always remember that. Sorry for your trouble. If I can ever be of service."

He handed Harry a business card which read: *Jimmy Malone, Finance and Loans. Quick and Confidential Service etc……………,* and quickly disappeared into the crowd.

Life afterwards improved financially at home, as Harry's father was well insured, and in less than a year his mother was regularly meeting another man. Harry never felt the same way about his mother again.

He himself had fallen for a dark haired beauty in College named Maura, who was studying Law. He proposed to her on a weekend trip to Paris on St. Valentine's Day, less than one month after his father was buried. They married six months later in Rome, in a small, private ceremony. His mother was not pleased by the timing and location of the wedding, but he didn't care.

His career progressed rapidly, and after three years he was made head of a new Department in the Bank, dealing in a range of new banking products. These involving the Bank speculating large sums of money on future movements of currencies, and interest rate swaps etc. He saw a lot of similarity here to gambling on horses (which he still indulged in over the internet, without Maura's knowledge); and he proved to be very successful in backing winners for the Bank.

They bought a detached, house on the hill of Howth, the year Maura gave birth to their second child, a beautiful girl, to accompany their two year old son. Harry was on top of the world, and felt nothing could go wrong. He was invited to give lectures all over Europe by the bank, detailing how he had achieved his outstanding results. He was feted, and invited to lavish dinners and parties. He found work taking up more of his time, and he began to see less of his family. He tried to compensate by bringing them on expensive holidays to exotic places. And buying Maura designer clothes, and a top-of - the range family car. Maura felt that his long working day and trips abroad were a price they both had to pay, in the short term, for the future of their family.

Harry had kept his apartment near the office, and it was very convenient sometimes to use it, rather than travel home, after a late meeting or business dinner. And he also found it useful, if he fancied inviting a pretty female from the office, or one visiting, back for a private drink, and maybe sometimes to stay the night! He felt it was a little reward for his hard work.

He quite liked the thrill of the chase with women, and his lifestyle gave him many opportunities. But one beautiful girl he met in London, quite knocked him out. She was a twenty year old Brazilian beauty named Nadia, who was a dancer in a Soho night club. She hoped to make enough money in two years in London, to return and settle down in Rio. She had an easy gracefulness about her, and Harry arranged trips to London as often as he could. He liked to lavish her with expensive gifts, and money. His life was now a roller-coaster, and he wasn't getting off! *He had it made.*

A year after he met Nadia, things started to unravel. *September 11th* had happened, and the financial markets were in turmoil. He was suddenly facing enormous losses in his investment portfolios in the Bank. His huge annual performance bonuses were wiped out overnight. He had already borrowed, and spent the money. He tried to cover up the losses by falsifying documents to buy more time to recover. The Bank's internal controls and senior management were poor, and this was quite easily done. Unfortunately this gambling strategy only led to a worsening of the Bank's financial position. Six months later, he realised that his hidden losses were so big, that the whole future of the Bank was in danger. He was working late every week in his apartment, and the pressure was affecting his relationship with Maura and his family. He found it hard to sleep at night, and dreaded going into the office each day to discover nothing had changed. The only place he found relaxing was the pub; or a trip to London, which was now a rare event.

There was a re-shuffle in the top management in the Bank, and within weeks he heard that there would be a comprehensive internal audit of his department, at an unspecified date. He realised that his time had run out, and he was facing total ruin. He also had a threatening phone call from Jimmy Malone. He was considerably in arrears in his repayments on loans to fund his gambling losses on the internet.

"Sure Jimmy, no problem, you'll have your money next week. I give you my word."

"You said that last time, kid. Only because of your father, I'll give you one last chance. Screw up, and you'll be sorry. Very sorry."

"Thanks Jimmy, you won't regret it."

He replaced the receiver, his hand shaking, knowing he had no chance of honouring his promise. The following night he had a phone call from London. It was Nadia. Crying.

"Harry, I've just found out that I'm pregnant! I didn't know what to do, so I had to ring you".

"I…..I'm glad you did, darling. Don't panic. I can't speak now, as I have visitors. But I'm going to London next week, and we can discuss the matter properly then. Thanks for letting me know."

He *had* thought things couldn't possibly get any worse. Now *this*. A cold sweat broke out on his brow. He reached for the vodka bottle.

In summer, depending on the weather, he often left the house early, went for a jog, and a swim, and then continued on into the office. This morning, he parked the car in his usual place, near the steps leading down the rocks to the sea. His pin stripe suit lay neatly folded on the back seat of the car.

Dressed in his track suit and running shoes, he stood with the half empty vodka bottle, gazing into the deep.

He checked that there no one around, and walked to the cliff edge, and threw the bottle onto the rocks below, smashing it completely. *Has to look like an accident, at least Maura will have the house.*

He then took off his track suit, and placed it folded on the grass, with his running shoes on top, and dressed only in his bathing shorts, walked slowly to the edge of the cliff. A cyclist passed, and waved a greeting. Harry waved back. *Perfect* .When the cyclist disappeared, he whispered, *goodbye.* A black raven flapped down onto a nearby waste basket, and stared at him with its head held down at an angle. Harry felt a shiver run up his back, as he returned the bird's beady stare.

He ran back to the car, took out, and donned a new track suit he had bought the previous day. He also took out a rucksack, containing casual clothes and shoes. He placed the car keys with his old track suit on the grass.

Putting the rucksack on his back, he headed off at a brisk pace towards Dublin. In a few hours, complete with the clothing, cash, and new fake passport and ID papers, he would rendezvous in London with Nadia, and they would fly to Brazil, to start a new life together. To become yet another person, like Lord Lucan, who vanished mysteriously without trace. *There's always another day,* he thought, smiling, as he boarded the plane.

Holy Orders

The humidity was the worst. Excess heat I could handle, but when the beads of perspiration became a river down the back of my neck! I ran from the car in the white hot heat to ring the bell at Miriam's villa. No answer. Back to the car's coolness. Temperature gauge read early forties. Typical Abu Dhabi July! Switched AC to maximum. Watch read two twenty five. Twenty five minutes late already! I guess it's a woman's privilege to be late for her own wedding. But it was not like Miriam. Solid as a rock. Dependable.

A car pulled up at the villa. It was the Best Man, Greg Peters. An Aussie. He rang the bell. No answer. He was startled by a large ghekko scampering up the wall beside him. He turned and ran to my car. I let down the window.

"What's the story mate? Where's Miriam?"

"Damned if I know. I've been here over 30 minutes. Women!"

"I'd better head on then mate, to the church and tell them to relax, and expect a delay."

"Yeah, Greg, you hightail it to the church. We shouldn't be too long." I let up the window.

I flicked on the radio. *Desert Island Discs*. Great, one my favourites. Still going in the nineties, it has stood the test of time! Just the job to while away the minutes.

Maybe they'll play *Get Me To The Church On Time*! Abu Dhabi was a long way from Mayo, for Miriam on her big day. Grant too, him being an Aussie. Melbourne. Me, I was sort of chuffed at being chauffeur, and stand-in father of the bride. Now, that's another story. I closed my eyes and my mind drifted.

Miriam was a nurse in the *Sheikh Salman* Maternity Hospital. We met playing tennis for the Irish Society. I was subbed in one day against the Indian club, and I became her regular, long-in-the-tooth partner. I quickly twigged that where there's a man/woman combo, the opposition tend to target the lady in question. However, if ever I "poached" a return heading into her quarter, as I was wont to do, I was quickly put in my place. No big row. Just a shrug. And a quiet "That was mine!" She was calm under pressure too! *And* capable. We played third string on the team, but often punched above our weight in the matches. I guess we understood each other.

We had a barbeque one night in our villa, for the Irish Tennis team. Miriam and Grant on the sofa. Me talking to them for a long time. The party almost finished. She made to playfully punch me in the face, for excessive "poaching" in the last match against the British Club. Then I copped it. A large diamond cluster ring. Engagement.

"Congratulations partner, why didn't you say so earlier?"

"Well I thought you'd never notice."

The party ended on a high note. Wedding to be six months later in June. Said she would be too busy to play tennis in the coming months. I didn't realise there was that much to planning a wedding! Anyway best not to take a chance on an injury!

About six weeks before the wedding day Miriam rang. Said her folks couldn't make it to the wedding. Got a shock when she asked would I do the father –of – bride role. Said I'd be delighted and honoured. Of course.

"And where's the ceremony?"

"In the grounds of *Sheikh Salman* hospital. There's a small, inter-denominational church there. Some of the staff might like to come over for a few minutes. *Father Ignacio* will do the ceremony. Though he wasn't too happy with it not being held downtown in *his* church."

"Really? Why?"

"I don't know for sure. His church is catholic but it's too big; and inconvenient. Anyway, it's my call. But he's such a *bully*. I'm worried in case something goes wrong on the day."

"Everything will be fine. Don't worry."

"You're right. There's enough other things to think about. Thanks anyway, I really appreciate you doing it."

"My pleasure Miriam."

I put down the phone. *Father Ignacio*. I suppose it had to be him. No choice. Rumour had it he was a traffic cop in Bombay, before a bolt of lightning struck. Or a career change, Holy Orders, beckoned. Anyone who attended Mass in his church would know that he brought his penchant for ordering traffic about, with him. His sermons went on endlessly as he harangued the poor Indian and Philipino audiences about their lack of faith and Christianity, and threatened all sorts of hell and damnation on their heads. I wondered would he adopt a similar attitude to an all-white congregation.

I woke to hear a car horn blasting, and an excited high pitched babble of voices. I looked out the car window. Miriam's car had pulled up outside her villa. *At last*. I looked at my watch. Three fifteen. Hell's bells! And she still had to get dressed! I hailed Angela, the bridesmaid who was following Miriam into the villa.

"Angela, did something awful happen? Where *were* you since eleven o'clock?"

"At the hairdresser's. We were at the hairdresser's."

"You must be joking."

"No, I'm not joking."

"What happened then?"

"We had an appointment for eleven. But just as we were about to go in, *Sheik Salman's* wife and entourage arrived."

"Had she an appointment?"

"No."

"And?"

"Well, we just had to wait. She *is* the *Sheikh*'s wife you know. This *is* the Middle East."

"I suppose. Did her hair even look beautiful after jumping the queue?

"I don't know, she was wearing her *abiya*. She had her hands hennaed as well, to add to the delay. Of all the bad luck…..I better get in and help Miriam dress."

"*Please*. It's nearly three thirty."

I pulled the car as near the villa gate as I could and waited. Two Arabian ladies passed the villa sheltering from the sun under a black umbrella. After about fifteen minutes the bridal party emerged and bundled into the back of the car. We had gone five minutes when Angela screamed:

"*Jesus,* stop the car."

"Ok. What is it now?"

"The flowers."

"The flowers?"

"We forgot the flowers. They're back in the villa."

I held my breath, and did a quick u-turn. We retrieved the flowers, and headed once more for the *Sheikh Salman* compound. There was a tense silence inside the car. The hot wind was whipping up little twisters in the desert sands outside beyond the highway.

I decided to take a short cut and enter by a gate at the rear of the compound. When we got there the gate was locked.

"Sorry about that ladies, another fine mess! We're late anyway. Might as well be hung for a sheep as a lamb."

"Ok, but you better move it, I'm a bit worried about *Father Ignacio*."

We moved fast along the highway, beside the numerous "nodding donkeys" obediently probing beneath the desert sands for black gold. Saw Arab families parking their cars along the side of the highway; and placing their prayer mats towards Mecca. It was *Saladh*. Prayer time. Finally the little church came into view. It was four thirty. I took Miriam's hand. It was shaking. She looked quite beautiful. I told her so. We walked up under the long canopy leading from the road to the church door. Even under its shelter the heat was searing. There was a small group outside the church headed by *Father Ignacio*. His face was impassive and he removed his glasses which had steamed up, and he commenced wiping them. A young Indian altar boy fanned him from the heat. Before we could say anything he spoke:

"I cannot say the Mass. We will just do the wedding ceremony."

I looked at Miriam. There were tears in her eyes. And her make-up was starting to stream down her face from the heat under the awning. She said:

124

"Why can you not say the Mass? Is it because we are late? I'm not having my wedding ceremony *without* the Mass. And that's final! I'm not taking orders from *you!*"

Father Ignacio seemed taken aback by her reply. I decided to step in.

"What exactly is the problem then, *Father Ignacio?*"

"We cannot get into the sacristy to get the chalice and vestments needed to say Mass."

"Why?"

"The key is apparently missing." The contemptuous tone was apparent.

Greg, the best man, came out of the church door.

"Problems mate. The guy with the key is missing. We're searching high and low. We think he's at work. He takes it with him as the church is shared with different denominations. He lives on the compound but his house is empty. We've just got his work number."

I realised that Father Ignacio could have solved the problem long ago by getting the missing items from his *own* church; but I decided avoid confrontation, and find another remedy.

"*Father Ignacio*, could we not just get some bread and a bottle of wine, and you could say Mass then?"

"No."

"Why?"

"Because they are not consecrated."

His negativity was frustrating, and I held myself back with difficulty. I looked at Miriam. Her calmness in the sweltering heat under the canopy was admirable. Although I could see tears welling in her eyes.

"Won't be too long now, Miriam."I said, more in hope than anything. She nodded.

And it wasn't long as Greg arrived just then, key in hand.

We proceeded indoors into the packed church, and up the aisle, where I handed Miriam over to a relieved Grant.

"Thanks mate." I was quite relieved to finally have finally reached this point but it wasn't all over yet.

Just at the critical point when Miriam was placing the ring on Grant's finger a mobile phone loudly bleeped on the altar. And continued. Eventually *Father Ignacio* struggled underneath his vestments one-handed, as he was holding a book in the other, and produced the offending mobile. He was taken aback by this incident, and thrust the phone into the hands of the young Indian altar boy, indicating for him to switch it off. The boy was equally flustered, and obviously not familiar with these new fangled gadgets. He pressed numerous buttons but the phone continued to ring. Father Ignacio snapped. His orders were being disobeyed again. He placed the book on the altar, took the phone, and slapped the altar boy on the cheek at the same time with his other hand. He then switched it off and replaced it in his vestments, and continued the ceremony as if nothing had happened.

Happily things went normally at the church thereafter. *Father Ignacio* did not linger long.

We eventually travelled to the hotel, to commence the celebrations. The best man read out the congratulatory letters and cards. After the usual speeches, Miriam surprised us all by announcing that she wanted to speak. This was not normally her style. When she stood up, and flicked back her veil over her head, and hitched up her white, flowing dress, I was struck by her calmness and beauty, after what must have been a difficult day for her.

"This is the happiest day of my life. Everything was wonderful about it for me. I hope it was for Grant too. Neither of us could have our families here to share our joy. But we have someone here, for you to meet, who's far more important to us."

Then Grant appeared from behind a screen, and handed her a little bundle of joy, that we were informed later was two month old Maeve. Born on the first of May. In *Sheikh Salman's* hospital of course. A lot of things then fitted into place. The congratulations and celebrating were even greater after this happy news.

Later, when dancing I asked Miriam if *Father Ignacio* would be performing the christening. She smiled.

"I think not, Bill. I think it will be in Ireland. I 'm sure my family would like that."

Mindin' the Kids

    I suppose Dun Laoghaire wasn't the worst place to grow up in after the war. It wasn't the best either. We lived on the main street, with two bedrooms upstairs. There was a small yard at the back of our house, with the lav at the end of it. Behind the yard was a slaughterhouse, and the tomcats patrolled the yard wall, mewling at all hours. Upstairs the rooms were lit by gas in a ghost light.

    The trams clanged by our front door, sparks sizzling overhead. Some had no roof on top, and when it rained there would be a mad scarper downstairs. The trams had seats that could face front ways or back ways. I wanted to be a tram conductor, clicking tickets, when I grew up, and one Christmas I got a conductor set from Santa. Santa knew everything. Me Da told me once that when me young brother was born he went with me ma at five in the morning into the Rotunda hospital on the tram.

    Next door was a pub called *Cheerio's?* A speak easy. There was a laneway at the back leading onto York Road. An escape way for people drinking after hours, if there was a raid by the cops. People would stand outside our house when the pub was closed, and when the coast was clear, knock on the pub door. The owner would peek out behind the blinds, and if he knew the guy, exchange signs, and let him in. People used stagger out'v the pub onto the street late at night, clutching brown paper parcels of stout, and singing their heads off. There was one guy who used drink there, he sticks in me memory. He was a lanky beanpole of a guy, all dressed in white with white hat and red dickybow, and a white poodle in tow. He was always three sheets to the wind. Sometimes four or five. He fell off the tram outside our door one day. His name was *Lennox Robinson*, and he was supposed to be some class of a writer. One night me Da had one over the eight in Cheerio's, and got sick in the lav in the pub. Funny thing, the next day his false teeth had vanished!

Across the road was a small sweetshop called *Howgegoe's*. Funny name. Welsh. They were an old couple. He was a bit grumpy, but she was a kindly lady, and sometimes gave you a little extra for your pennyworth. The sweets were all in row on the counter in large jars. *Bonbons, Bullseyes, Lime Lemon and Acid, Liquorice Allsorts*, and *Conversation lozenges*. Forbidden fruit. I used dream of nicking into the shop and grabbin' a handful of sweets, and leggin' it down the street, before the old man came out from the backroom. But he was too smart. He had a bell on the shop door. So I chickened out. Me older brother dared me one day, so I opened the shop door and shouted in " How did it go , Mister Howgegoe", and belted around the corner.

Beside the sweetshop was *Masseys,* the undertakers. The sign in their window said they gave you a complete funeral service, and would never let you down! Next door to them was a shoemender's shop. He used to put steel studs in me boots to make the leather last longer. After I would slide me boots on the concrete to see if the sparks would fly! When he was puttin' on a leather sole, I couldn't believe it when he took the tacks out of his mouth, like a magician. And he would wax the string like some strange snake before threadin' it in the awl when stitchin' me shoes. On the corner of York Road was another shop called "Florrie's". She was a dark haired, jolly lady. Middle aged, good looking. The dockers and sailors would hang around her window in the afternoon sun, and shoot the breeze with her. She sold delicious cream buns from *Johnston Mooney's*, and you could get a bag of broken biscuits for only tuppence. One of the guys who hung around her shop was Dummy Dawmer. Everyone knew him and we all felt sorry for him. He sold evening papers outsideWoolies.EVENINHERALDERMAIL.EVENIN HERALDERMAIL.

There were three coal merchants near us.*Tedcastles, Heitons, and McCormicks*. The coal was delivered sometimes on horse drawn carts. The coal porters were like black and white minstrels, humpin' the coal into the houses, and sometimes one might do an *Al Jolson* song if the mood was on him. *Swanee* or *Mammee*. If any coal fell off onto the street, it was quickly snaffled up into one of the houses close by. A lot of houses left their doors open all the time. After the war it was mostly Polish coal, full of stones and damp slack. Tryin' to light the fire everyday was like tryin' to launch the *Queen Mary*. Lots of sticks and newspapers, and then a page of the newspaper across the fire to draw the flames. As the fire began to take, a black spot would appear on the page, slowly getting bigger, until it went on fire, and *whoosh,* the paper vanished up the chimney!

I liked nicking into Woolies on the way to school, just to look at the toy cowboys and Indians, and soldiers, and all the goodies. No money, just looking. There was a small shop near the Library, that had a one armed bandit that took pennies. I luv'd the thrill of winning even a penny. Made me day. Past the Church were three big shops all in a row, *Payantake's, Home & Colonial, and Lipton's*. I would stare through the window in *Liptons* for ages, at the wonderful machine flying like a cablecar through the air up to the cash office and back with the money!

Me dad was a butcher, and cycled to work in Blackrock everyday 'cept Sundays. He cycled home for dinner too. Sometimes he'd have an accident in work. I hated to see the white bandages on his hand with the red splotches of blood seepin' through on his fingers. I hated blood. Yuck! But we never starved. Even with the rationin'! Me dad built a seat on the crossbar of his bike, so he could carry me'n me brother on the carrier at the same time. One day me dad was flying down the hill at Seapoint back to work, when a man goin' by on a motorbike yelled at him:

"Hey mister, you're on fire!"

He looked down, and he'd put his lit pipe in his top pocket, and it'd burnt through to his woollen jersey, trailing smoke behind like a ship. After that me ma used call him *Steamboat Bill*!

Across the road, there was a laneway between *Howgegoe's* shop and *Smyth's* pub that led to a large waste ground beside the corpo rubbish tip, near the Fire Station. Here we hung around and played in gangs, the live long day, right through the year. There was a season for marbles and conkers. We played football against the wall in the winter, and in the summer painted three stumps on the wall, for the wicket, and played cricket, with a piece of wood for the bat! We used box the fox every year in the luscious orchard behind the Town Hall .The girls played hopscotch on the path there, and swung round the poles on ropes, and skipped, singin':

A drip a drop the robbers on the sea,
My o my they're after me,
Are you going to the fair?
I went to the fair and I went,
But the fair's not there

The older girls played chasing with the boys, and when they were caught, would scream as the older boys tried to kiss them! We thought those were *silly* games.

If a bin lorry went in to empty its stinking rubbish into the incinerator, in the corpo dump we'd hold our noses, and sneak in unbeknowns, for a gawk. The flames would flare up the huge chimney stack. Like *Dante's* bleeding inferno! If we were spotted the corpo men would chase after us. We loved the chase! At the fire station we'd sometimes try to shimmy up the firemen's pole, but it was too shiny to grip. We were dying to see them come tumbling down, like in a real alarm. But we never did. I wondered if they put grease on their hands and if they all fell on top of each other on the floor like the firemen in the *Keystone Cops* movies. And if they got a thrill coming down all that way on their bums, at such speed!

Other times we'd get thru a gap in the bars and cross the railway line to play cowboys and Indians at the Gut in *Salthill,* and at the huge metal buoys beside the green at the harbour. We'd watch the trains shunting wagons on the railway line up through the buoys. Me da told me that the coal shovel would be so hot the driver and stoker could fry their breakfast on it! The great *Iron Horse* hissing steam at the Indians. *White man speak with forked tongue. Only good Indian is a dead Indian.*

White man try to kill Indian. Indian live. White man kill buffalo. Indian die. Sometimes I'd be *Geronimo* or *Cochise, Crazy Horse, or Sitting Bull* or sometimes *Kit Carson, Gene Autry, Roy Rogers(duck-the –bullet), Hopalong Cassidy,* or *Billy the Kid.* But the Indians always ended up getting shot. We played in the summer in the People's park, when the flowers were all out an' smelling sweet. But the Ranger made sure football was out. There was a tap in the park and you could drink the water from an iron cup on a chain. The water always tasted so lovely and cool from the metal cup. Like from a metal chalice!

    The thing I luv'd best of all was going to the flicks. There were four cinemas near us. The *Pavilion* (the Pav or fleapit we called it) at the end of Marine Road. In Glasthule the *Astoria,* where every Saturday they had a trailer (or follyerupper) which lasted ten minutes and always ended with the hero (*Superman, Batman, Dick Tracy, Congo Bill, or Nyoko of the Jungle*) in mortal danger. So you had to go back the next week to see if they made it. Thanks be to god they always did! Then there was the *Picture House* at the corner of Mulgrave Street, which only showed *Walt Disney* cartoons. *Micky Mouse, Donald Duck, Goofy, and Pluto etc.* The show here only lasted an hour and a half, and when it was over I'd sometimes hide under the seat to see it again without payin'! Lastly there was the Adelphi, which was huge, but if *Tarzan* was on, the queues were for miles, and you mightn't get in. I hated when that happened. I loved *Laurel and Hardy* flicks; and any war or western ones. Or anything with *John Wayne* in it. *He* was my hero, the hell he was, whether sorting out the Japs in *Flying Tigers*; or the Indians in *Stagecoach.*

The only problem with going to the flicks was money. That was scarce as hen's teeth in those days. From seven years on, me and me older brother used mind the kids for me ma. So she could have a break and stick her head in a book. Usually we'd take them for a walk in the pram for a few hours, and earn a few pence. This meant more chances to get to the flicks.

Me younger brother in the pram had been very sick when he was born, and was always cranky, an' bawlin'. The only thing that cheered him up was the steam trains or "*Puff puffs*", as he called them. Sometimes a kind old lady would feel sorry for him and give us a penny to buy him a lollipop. One day I was mindin' me kid brother when I joined up with my older brother and a gang at the railway bridge on Crofton Road. There was a grass top on the bridge, and you could climb onto it, and look down on the trains passing by underneath, and the steamy soot would come up and blacken your face like an Indian. I parked the pram up against a lampost at the top of the hill, and climbed up onto the bridge. We were going to drop small stones into the funnel of the train as it went by underneath. As I climbing up me older brother nicked me lollipop out of me pocket.

"Gimme that back, or I'll burst ye." I roared at him.

"Yeh, you an' what bleedin' army?" He shouted back.

"I'm warning ye, gimme it or I'll be dug outta ye." I yelled back.

He just laughed, so I lunged at him, and we ended up wrestling on top of the bridge just as the train steamed by underneath. Me little brother was roaring in the pram, so I had to jump down off the bridge. An old lady had arrived on the scene, and she gave us a telling off about not mindin' me baby brother better. Afterwards a young girl from the country came to live with us, and her job was to mind the kids for me ma. She got free lodgings and a few bob a week. We now had more time to play, but less money for the flicks!

On the day in question, I had gone to the Pav, with me mate Joey Dodd. I was steeped. The man had come to empty the gas meter that day, and me ma had got some cash back. So I was able to scrounge the price of the flicks off her. *John Wayne* was starring in *The Sands of Iwo Jima*. Couldn't wait to see it! We came out later into a sunny June evening with the Town Hall clock showing six o'clock, and the *Angelus* bells ringin' from *St. Michael's* church. It was a great movie but I was gutted! *John Wayne*, playing *Sergeant Ryker*, was shot in the back, at the very end, by a snipin' jap, just as he was having a drag, and saying that he never felt better in his whole life. I couldn't believe it. *John Wayne* was dead! *John Wayne* had bit the dust! Me whole life was upside down!

There was a water tap on the platform of the railway station in *Dun Laoghaire*. Funny, it was under a big sign on the station wall that said *Kingstown*. It had a metal cup on a chain, just like in the People's Park. We decided to go over to the station for a drink, to steady our nerves after the big shock. We crossed Marine Road, and walked down the steps onto the platform. A train had just pulled in as I lifted the metal cup to me lips, and knocked it back. The water was cool and clean, and I began to feel better straight away. I turned to head back up the railway steps when I froze. Coming down the steps holding the banister was me four year old brother, with his head of blondy curls blowin' in the wind. All on his own, and heading in the direction of the train. I grabbed him by the hand, and brought him straight home with me. Me ma was in bits, but when we arrived home her eyes lit up, and she grabbed him up into her arms.

"Where have you been alannah? I've been storming heaven all afternoon for you. My prayers have been answered." She cried as she hugged him and kissed him, and said she knew now how Mary felt when Jesus was lost in the Temple, and found again.

Me dad was out on his bike scourin' the town, with the cops, the whole afternoon. I had to walk to police station to tell them me brother was found. The girl from the country was mindin' him and me other brother in the pram on the pier when she lost him. That's what *she* said. I think she was probably looking into a shop window when it happened. As I was walking home, I started to wonder if I might get me old job of mindin' the kids back again. And get to the flicks more often. Yeh, great!

The Wedding

After long months of meticulous planning and heartache, less than a day remained. The arguments over the wedding dinner seat placings were the worst. Mary Ward sighed, and thought that after all that hassle, her married relationship was bound to be all the stronger. Whenever she felt really low, she would sneak a look into the wardrobe at her wedding dress. Then she felt better. Then she would light a cigarette and check all the arrangements again in her mind. For the umpteenth time. Sometimes she would glance at her two year old diamond cluster engagement ring. That too made her feel good inside. It made her feel secure that Arthur *really* loved her.

Her mind drifted back to when she first met Arthur Sampson, five years earlier. She was twenty years old, and had gone with a few friends from the factory to see the *Royal Showband* in the *Crystal Ballroom*. Normally, they didn't dance, but stood around the stage, eyes glued on *Brendan Bowyer's* gyrating hips. But when the tall, gangly, dark haired Arthur asked her to dance the *Hucklebuck*, she immediately accepted, to her own surprise. After the dance he invited her to have a drink at the bar. They introduced themselves, sipping minerals:

"Hey Mary, you're some mover, where'd you learn to dance so good?"

"I've always loved to dance. I've a rake of cups and things for Irish dancing. My ma brought me to every Feis Ceoil since I could walk. Then I did ballroom dancing in *Morosini Whelan's*. I'd love to be a Ballet Dancer like Dame *Margot Fontaine*. I'm taking ballet lessons now."

"Fair play to you."

"Where do you live, Arthur?

"Drimnagh. And you?

"Just down the road in Crumlin. And what do you do, may I ask? "

"You may. I've applied to join the Garda. Just like my father. I play the clarinet. I'm going to have my own band."

"Then why join the guards?

"I'll play in the Garda band, and get some experience first. Musically, that is. Then I'll leave and set up my own outfit.

"Oh, so you're going into the showband business, are you? Like the Royal?" she giggled.

"No, my band is going to be like Arty Shaw's. Big band style. He's my hero. When he plays *Begin the Beguine*, on his clarinet you're taken to another place. And women, they just go weak at the knees! You know he was married eight times!"

"Not really. How did you get to the *Crystal*?" she said, switching the topic.

"On my trusty Honda 50. How about you?"

"Shanks mare, I'm afraid. No luxuries for a Crumlin lass like me."

"Well, can I leave you home later?" he replied.

"I'll think about it. Thanks."

She did, and he did leave her home that night. And they became an item. And the relationship blossomed, although Arthur never formed his *Arty Shaw* band. But he played clarinet in the Garda band. And dreamed.

Everything is now in the hands of the gods, she sighed, thinking again of the wedding day. Her father was paying for everything. This worried her, as he would also have to pay later for her two younger sisters, her bridesmaids, when they got married.

A knock on the door. Her mother looked in.

"You alright love?"

"Sure mam, I'm fine."

"Don't worry Mary, everything will go well tomorrow. Try and have an early night. I've put the *Child of Prague* in the window. I'll say a prayer as well for the weather. Your father will be picking you up at 11.30; and you know all that has to happen before then."

"Ok, I know. I'll be ready. Thanks mam."

As the door closed she glanced at the clock. Ten. Better get ready to retire. But how will I ever get to sleep, with all those things to worry about? The jangling telephone interrupted her thoughts. It was Arthur.

"Mary, I want to call off the wedding tomorrow."

"What! Is this some sick joke? What are you thinking of, Arthur Sampson to say such a thing on the eve of our wedding? It's not one bit funny." She sobbed into the phone.

"It's not a joke, Mary. I *mean* it. I do *not* want to get married. And that's it."

"But why?" she spoke frantically, thinking she would suddenly wake up from this nightmare.

"No why. I've just thought it out long and hard, and that's my decision. I'm sorry to spring it on you so late, but that's it."

"No, that's not it. You've got to be kidding. We've had our moments, like everyone else. No big deal. But, but….. is there another woman?" Suddenly reality began to sink in. He *was* serious. Deadly serious.

"No, there's no one else involved. It's *my* decision. You're the only one who knows. Do I make myself clear? You *will* go to the church in the morning, and I *will not* show up. You can put all the blame on me." She detected a rising exasperation in his tone.

"Ok, if that's the way you want it." She placed the phone back on the receiver, in a daze, and sank down onto her bed, and cried. And cried. And fell asleep.

She woke up about an hour later, rushed to the bathroom, and looked in the mirror. The red rings around her eyes confirmed her worst fears. She looked ghastly. She walked to the wardrobe, and glanced at her wedding dress. Still the knot in her stomach and the pounding in her head. She lit a cigarette, and paced the floor, until she felt dizzy.

Jesus wept. How could this be happening to me? What am I going to do? My father will have a heart attack for sure. She walked to the window, looked out and saw the kids still kicking football under the pale hue of the streetlight, at the end of the front garden. Lucky them. Not a care in the world. Don't panic. Nobody's dead. *Yet*. She lit another cigarette.

It was past midnight when she rang him.

"Arthur, it's me, I need to talk to you."

"Mary, there's nothing further to discuss. My mind's made up. That's all there is to it." His voice had an irritated tone.

"Ok. I accept now that you've made your decision. But I just want to ask one favour. *Please.*" Her voice was trembling slightly.

"That depends. What's the favour?"

"Well, it's about tomorrow. Instead of me going to the church, and *you* not showing, I'd rather if you went to the church, and *I* didn't arrive. I'm worried about my father's health, and how the shock might affect him. Anyway, you owe me one, Arthur. Will you?"

"Sure Mary, I'll do it your way. It's the least I can do. I know it's been a big shock for you. Goodbye." Arthur replied, and put down the phone.

The sun was shining from a clear blue sky, as Arthur walked up and down outside the church. He looked at his watch. Five minutes to twelve. He walked down the huge barn-like church, and sat down at the communion aisle. Father Kelly adjusted his vestments, and came over.

"Don't worry Arthur, everything will be fine. I've seen that worried look on many a bridegroom's face. It's the waiting that makes you nervous. The ladies like to turn up late, but they always show up. On that you can rely. You can be sure everything would start on time if the roles were reversed."

"I suppose you're right there Father." Arthur replied, wishing secretly the priest would go away.

He heard a movement beside him, and turned. It was his brother Sean, the best man, breathing hard.

"They're here. I can't believe it. On time." Sean muttered.

The organ commenced blasting out the *Wedding March*. All eyes backwards on the bride and her frail father faltering hand-in-hand up the aisle. A lot of oohs and aahs. Everyone agreed afterwards that they had never seen Mary look so stunning. Arthur felt so too. He was in a state of shock. She looked like a princess in her elegant dress and long trailing train. Golden curly locks framed her oval face. Her veil was back over her head and her expression serene. And beautiful. But it was only when she placed the ring on his finger, and he said "I do", that he looked straight into her dark brown eyes. And she looked back. And smiled.

    The glorious June colours in the hotel garden were sharpened by the slanting afternoon sunlight. When they entered the foyer of the hotel, the bride and groom had to pass under a gauntlet formed by the Garda Band. As they ducked under, the band were playing a big hit of the time, called *Love and Marriage*. Everything about the rest of the day was wonderful. Her father even gave a long speech, and thanked the Lord for letting him live to see such a happy day. Her mother cried tears of happiness, and said how it reminded her of her own wedding day. Father Kelly added his few words, and a blessing on the newly-wedded couple. Arthur made a short speech, saying how happy he was, and how beautiful Mary looked. But it was only later, when he took the stage and played *Begin the Beguine* on his clarinet, that Arthur Sampson really relaxed, and let himself go. And inwardly Mary did too, and she was happy for him.

    I will never forget the day my ailing mother told me the story of her wedding day, from her sick bed. I was dumbstruck.

    "Veronica, you're my oldest and dearest, and I trust you with all my heart. I had to tell someone. I couldn't bring it with me to the grave." She said breathing heavily.

    "But mom, it was a huge risk you took."

"Yes, I suppose it was. But having four beautiful children, including you, and a long and happy life was worth it." She smiled back.

"You must have laughed heartily with Dad later, about his cold feet."

"No. We never discussed it."

"What! Never? I don't believe it."

"No. Never. He never brought it up. And neither did I."

"It was as if it never happened then?"

"I suppose you could say he just re-wrote history. Sometimes people have to do that to cope. I knew he was happy. He told me so, many, many times. He was a good husband, and he made me very happy. I couldn't have asked for more. We understood each other."

'But Mom, there's one question I'd like to ask, if you don't mind."

"Of course darling, what is it that's worrying you?"

"Well, how did you decide to do what you did, and then have the strength to go through with it? It needed a lot not to panic, and keep cool. *How* did you do it?"

Her mother paused, and after a few moments she replied in a slow, wavering voice

"I just prayed. And I prayed. And I prayed to St. Veronica too. Then I fell asleep. When I woke up, it was as if an angel of the Lord had whispered in my ear what to do. Veronica, there's one favour I must ask of you." Her voice was gasping.

"Sure Mom, what is it?"

"Please don't say anything to your father about today.Or anyone else in the family. Promise?"

"Of course Mam, I will always respect your wishes."

She passed away two weeks later. My father was heartbroken, and my mother's dying wish went with her to the grave.

Belief

 Talk about a pressure week! Having to get the monthly accounts out by Friday to London. He could have done without the visit of the internal auditor the same week. The joys of working for a multinational, mused Jim Kelly as he sorted the internal memos and external mail on his desk. *And* he was short two staff, one on holidays, one sick with migraine. *And* the new computer system was giving teething troubles. *And* he was having difficulty getting monthly information from the store accounts manager; tricky one that, as she was having an illicit affair with the General Manager. *And* he was having problems getting one of his staff to deliver on time. *And* the tension in Dublin city centre, what with the IRA hunger strike in the North; he felt every parked car on the street could contain a bomb. *And* his wife was taking their oldest child to have her eyes tested. They wouldn't be seeing much of each other this week, with the inevitable overtime looming. Still, in the eighties in Ireland, he was happy to have a job, highly paid and taxed; better than the emigration trail! He jabbed the keyboard of his computer to pull up his month end Work Timetable. The secret of his work achievement! Nothing happened. He jabbed again. This time something happened. The message *System Failure, consult your Local Maintenance Engineer*, flashed on the screen. He picked up the phone, frustration building.

 Later he glanced out his office window at the concrete city skyline. Below, the trees were shedding their rusty leaves on a golden autumn evening. Above, the sunlight was shining through a gap in the clouds, like a heavenly apparition onto the rooftops. Like a miracle light! He would need a miracle to get everything finished on time this month end! The phone rang on his desk. It was his boss David Epstein from London.

"Hello David."

" Jim old chap, how are things in Dublin, we are hearing worrying reports?"

"Tense, David. IRA protest marches every day in the city centre in sympathy with the hunger strikers. Sales are down. Naturally."

"Naturally. It's a bad show. Look Jim old boy, this is the end of Quarter, I'd like a detailed analysis of the Irish results compared with last year and Budget; and a revised cash flow projection to yearend, if you don't mind; as well as the usual margin reconciliation, with the accounts package. I have to do a financial presentation to the Group Board. Don't forget the minutes of the last Irish Board Meeting. We need to meet soon with our Irish Bankers to discuss better terms and new facilities. Also can you come to London next Monday for two days for a European financial meeting on future strategy?"

"No problem David, I will arrange everything, and come back to you."

"Thank you Jim, I look forward to hearing from you."

"You're welcome David."

The internal audit would last the entire week. A report would issue later on the findings. The problem was that it was circulated to his boss and other senior executives in London. Not good for career prospects! Last year he was furious when what he deemed trivial items such as using a pencil, and tippex were commented on. This year there was a new auditor, Paul Murphy, who originally hailed from Ireland, and had settled in London and was married, with two children. He might get a more sympathetic report this year. The protocol was to bring the auditor to dinner one night during his visit.

Jim booked a table for two at *The Old Dublin* restaurant in Francis Street on the Thursday night. As he drove to the *Shelbourne* Hotel to pick up his guest, a news flash on the car radio stated that Bobby Sands had just died on hunger strike in the Maze prison in the North. A feeling of foreboding gripped him. When would it ever end? He knew things were now going to get a lot worse in Ireland, North and South.

Later, in the midst of a fine meal, and halfway through a bottle of *ChateauNeuf duPape,* they had both relaxed, and the conversation turned inevitably to the political situation:

"Paul, it must be difficult sometimes, you being Irish working in a large UK company, with all the IRA terrorist activities on the UK mainland."

"Yes it is sometimes. The *Mountbatten* massacre was the worst. I was genuinely ashamed to be Irish at *that* time. There was even a coolness in the air in the company. You could sense it. And everyone was *so* polite and nice. That only made it worse."

"And Bobby Sands?"

"Funny, I think he genuinely *believed* in his principles. Bound to lead to reprisals though, in the UK by the IRA. Maggie Thatcher is *not* for turning." Jim felt it was time to talk about something else.

"What part of Ireland did you grow up in?"

"Sligo. Yeats Country. Near Collooney. Went to London when I was 25 years. Met my wife in London, and we now live happily near her family in Surrey."

"Ever think of coming back to live in the old sod?"

"No. Everything is settled where we are. The kids' schools are nearby, and everything is nicely bedded down. Although I do get nostalgic when I visit my mother. She's invalided at home. She's very religious. She used to go to mass every day. Now she sits at home and says rosaries. Every time I see her she says she has been saying prayers for me and my family. I *am* touched by that. My father's long dead and my sister Annie looks after her."

"That's very interesting, and I suppose you've inherited her holy ways, and kept the flame burning in the UK?"

"Not really, I'm rather ashamed to say. Although I was an altar boy in my youth, and I suppose you could say I was a bit of a holy Joe. I remember once even going on an enclosed Retreat for three days, in my teens, and giving serious thought to the Priesthood. Of course my mother was pushing that, and would have been delighted if I had turned out a priest."

"And what made you decide not to?"

"I…..I had a sort of a dream during the Retreat. Decided it was a sign from God."

"Ah, divine intervention! And I presume that you still have the faith, but just don't bother to practise it in England, as you're outnumbered over there?"

"You presume wrong my friend. I *don't* have the faith any more. I am a non-believer." He lifted the wine glass to his lips.

"I must say I *am* surprised. And pray how did this *volte facie* come about? And after you being born and reared in the isle of saints and scholars. "

"It happened gradually. Once you got away from the claustrophobic catholic setup in rural Ireland…..I mean so many people I knew in Sligo went to mass on Sunday, only because they were afraid of what the neighbours would say!"

"There's truth in that, but there's many an Irish person who went to work in England, who found his religion a great comfort."

"Yes, I suppose. But I started reading a lot, Joyce, Sartre, and so on. Opened my mind."

"Do you believe in God?"

"No."

"And who then made the world? And how come we're spinning madly through space if there's no superior being?

"*Cause and effect.* Everything is governed by the law of cause and effect. I believe in Shakespeare's theory that *we are such stuff as dreams are made of, and our little life is rounded with a sleep."* He filled his glass to the brim, and toasted the absent bard.

"And your wife, is *she* a disciple of the cause and effect credo?" Jim's voice had a sardonic tinge.

"No. She's quite religious in fact, although of a different persuasion. And she makes the kids attend religious school every Sunday. I'm happy with that. We just don't discuss my beliefs. Or lack of. I'm very happy with my life, and I feel *completely* in control."

"Paul, would you believe it's nearly twelve? *Tempus fugit.* And I've a hectic schedule tomorrow. I'll get the tab."

"Please let me."

"Nonsense. You're in Ireland. You're my guest. It's all the one company."

"Ok, thanks Jim. Lovely place. I've had a great night. I feel that I've unburdened my soul. And I don't do that very often. God knows." He smiled at the inadvertent joke.

When they left the restaurant, and walked down Francis Street, past the closed, shuttered, antique shops, towards Thomas Street where the car was parked, a light mist began to fall, and the wind was blowing the dead rusted leaves before their feet. Jim was happy he had left the car in a secure, guarded car park. He immediately felt the tension on the streets of Dublin. Before they reached the car two urchins appeared out of the shadows. They were scruffily dressed and had their hands out begging. Paul said

"Jim, have you any change, I've only got sterling."

"Sure." He dropped some coins into the outstretched hands.

The next morning Jim was ticking off his Work Timetable on his desk. Two items outstanding. Predictable. Time was running out. He had until five o'clock. He would work around the problem. Make estimates, run off the figures, and start the analysis report. And pray the computer doesn't act up! The phone rang. It was Paul Murphy.

"Jim, sorry to disturb. I know today is *D* day for your month end. I have a problem. I……I can't seem to find my wallet. I've searched high and low here in the hotel. Sod's law I had taken cash from the bank yesterday, to give my mother when I visit her tomorrow. It may have fallen from my pocket when I was in your car last night. I wonder if you could have a look in your car." He sounded slightly shaken.

"Ok. My car is in the yard below. I'll run down and check; and ring you back straightaway. Stay in the hotel."

A few minutes later he rang the hotel.

"No luck I'm afraid, Paul."

"I was just thinking, those two beggars we met last night must have picked my pocket. It was quite easily done in the dark, with two of them. I had better go to the police."

"It's possible. But why don't you wait until ten o'clock, and take a taxi over to the restaurant, and check there, before you do that. The cleaners will be in the restaurant then."

"Ok, but it's not likely. After all you paid the bill." Paul's voice sounded forlorn. He certainly did *not* sound in control.

Jim was just getting his mind focussed on his report, when the phone rang again.

"Found it Jim. Under the dining table in the restaurant. Thanks be to God. It must have fallen out while we were talking. I remember now taking off my jacket to drape on the chair after the meal. It must have fallen out then." He sounded much relieved and much happier.

"Thanks be to God is right, Paul. So when *you* were expounding on your theory of cause and effect, somebody up there was having a right old laugh at your expense! What do you believe now, Paul? Was it just cause and effect, a pure coincidence, or divine intervention?"

"I…..I'm not sure. I'll have to think about it. I'll see you later." Jim then realised that Paul was quite moved by what had happened. Like he'd been touched on a raw nerve.

Anyway, this isn't getting the job finished. He turned back to his report.

Cuban Song

　　Back in the early sixties in Dublin, things weren't exactly swinging, but there was a lot going on. Musically, that is. On the pop scene, Elvis's star was slightly on the wane; and the Beatles had burst like a comet into the musical firmament of the world. The Irish Showband phenomenon was reaching its zenith. Irish traditional music was beginning a long road to global popularity with the Chieftains and other groups. Fleadh Ceol na hEireann was a major event in the Irish musical calendar.

　　My girlfriend Maggie and I were heavily into folk music, which was taking off in various clubs and pubs in the city. The spark that ignited a few years earlier in Greenwich Village, New York, where the Clancy Brothers started to sing rebel songs and songs of the Irish people, had kindled a flame that had fired the imagination of people everywhere. We never missed a concert of the Clancy Brothers and Tommy Makem in the National Stadium. Their success not only worked wonders for exports of Aran sweaters, but also encouraged other talented Irish musicians to perform publicly. Maeve Mulvany was the queen of the balladeers. Frank Harte sang old Dublin ballads from the time of Zozimus. Anne Byrne and Jessee Owens sang beautiful love duets. Luke Kelly lifted the rafters off the roof of the Green Cinema, where he performed in solo midnight concerts. The Dubliners began their long and successful career in O'Donoghue's pub etc etc. Maggie and I were off every Friday night to the International Bar in Wicklow Street to hear Johnny McEvoy. He always ended up with the rousing "New

York Girls", or the rollicking rebel song "The Merry Ploughboy", and had everyone singing their heads off, and yelling for more. The Abbey Tavern in Howth, The Embankment in Tallaght, and The Carney Arms in Dun Laoghaire were other folk venues where the craic was mighty.

"Hey Mags, have you heard the news? Pete Seeger's coming to town."

"Pete who?"

"Pete Seeger, it says here in the *Herald* he's one of the living legends of American folk music, and he's coming to Dublin for the first time in July to give a solo concert in the St Francis Xavier Hall."

"*So*, what's his claim to fame?"

"Well it seems he was a contemporary of Woody Guthrie and Leadbelly, and sings a lot of songs about social injustice, and he was blacklisted during the infamous McCarthy era in America. Sounds like there's a touch of Irish rebel blood somewhere in his veins. He's also in the vanguard of the civil rights movement sweeping through America just now. He's a virtuoso on the five string banjo and the guitar; and has sung with the famous Weavers. "*Goodnite Irene*"; and "*So long, it's been good to know you*" were their big hits. Need I go on?"

"No, but you better hurry and book the tickets."

Maggie was right. The concert sold out in no time. We arrived early, but there was still a big queue outside, with everyone anxious to get the best seats, as it was free seating inside.

"Gee Maggs, what an atmosphere! I sure hope the concert doesn't turn out a flop."

"I don't think so, Bobby. I see a lot of folk music aficionados in the audience. They know their stuff. In fact we might be in for a rare old evening."

Seeger took the stage alone, save for his various instruments, and a glass and pitcher of water on a small table. He was a lean-framed six footer, in his mid fifties, with high temples, and a sharp angular face, and spoke with a languid western drawl.

He predictably kicked off with a popular song of the day, which had communist overtones. It was called "*If I had a Hammer*". He followed that with the civil rights anthem" *We Shall Overcome*". In no time he had he had the audience in the palm of his hand. He was a supreme professional. He could work an audience like nobody else. He divided everyone into groups, and had them singing along in harmony on certain songs. With such unprecedented audience participation, the time flew by. Towards the end he sang a few songs written by one of best young folk song writers emerging in the United States. Bob Dylan. One was called "*A Hard Rain's A-Gonna Fall*", an apocalyptic poem-song of amazing imagery, which seemed to be about a nuclear fallout. Everyone was paranoid about such an event after the Cuban Missile Crisis the previous year. That night he championed the writer, but a few years later, at the Newport Folk Festival, when Dylan went electric for the second half of his gig, Seeger was so infuriated that he threatened to cut the electric cabling with an axe. Seeger was *true* to his folk roots.

   Seeger's final song was a haunting, lyrical melody of exquisite beauty and simplicity. It was partly in Spanish and was called "*Guantanamera*". With the whole audience joining in the chorus, the singer brought an unforgettable night to a wonderful conclusion. On the way home we were still humming the chorus of the tune. It had a way of getting into your head. And staying there. I read somewhere afterwards that Seeger had popularized this song in the States when he sang it in the Carnegie Hall in New York in early 1963, at a pro-Cuba solidarity concert. Many years later, a group called the Sandpipers had a number one hit worldwide with the tune. At this time I began to remember more of the English translation of the song which started "*I am a peaceful man from the land of the palm trees.........*"

   Forty years later, my wife Maggie and I alighted in *Jose Marti* Airport, Havana, on a sweltering February afternoon. It was our first holiday in Cuba, and was partly due to having seen the wonderful Ry Cooder – inspired movie "*The Buona Vista Social Club*", the previous year. Cooder is one of the foremost slide guitar players in the world, and Cuba the country where African drum beats and Spanish guitar strings fused together to produce the most pulsating rhythms imaginable.

   "The airport's a bit dilapidated, Bob. No proper air conditioning. I suppose that's what you get in a communist regime. And who the heck is *Jose Marti* ?"

"Yeah, it *is* a bit run down. No Russian money any more. Must be difficult to manage here, with the American economic blockade. But I can tell you a little about *Jose Marti* from what I've just read in the inflight magazine. He was a revolutionary poet, killed in a freedom fight in the late nineteenth century."

"It's impressive that the capital city's airport is called after a poet, and not the local dictator. Why don't we do something original like that in Ireland?"

"Good question."

I later learned that the words of one of Marti's famous poems were used in the song "*Guantanamera*". Marti was from a beautiful maritime place in the south of the island called Guantanamo, which inspired the poem. Pretty soon I realized that the song was literally the national anthem of Cuba, as it featured in the repertoire of every Cuban musician serenading in the pubs and restaurants of the hotels. When I heard the enchanting melody, I pictured a long white coral shoreline with elegant palm trees gracefully swaying in the wind, in time with the music. I was curious to learn more about Jose Marti.

A few days later, I arrived late on the hot-baked beach to find Maggie esconced under an umbrella, with a book in one hand, and a *Mojito* in the other.

"Hi Bob, what kept you? You should try one of these *Mojitos*. They're just the job for the heat. Mint flavoured. *Hemingway's* recipe."

"I was looking up something on the Internet, What's the book like?"

"Great. I'm really enjoying it. It's about a girl who was murdered, and tells the story from Heaven."

"Really?"

"Yes, really. Is there something on your mind Bob? You look worried."

"Well, there is actually. I keyed in the word Guantanamo on the net, to get more information on *Jose Marti's* birthplace, and got a lot of unexpected and disturbing stuff instead."

"What kind of stuff?"

"Apparently a part of Guantanamo Bay has been leased to America from way back. It's been used for the past few years as a prison for nearly 600 Islamic militants."

"Yes Bob, I've read something to that effect. I suppose they're entitled to use it for whatever purpose they like, if they're paying for it."

"But these people are only suspects, and are imprisoned indefinitely without trial, against all human and civil rights laws. They're clothed in orange-coloured uniforms, and kept manacled in tiny wire cages. And put under a daily system of mental torture and interrogation, to breakdown their minds and make them confess to the crimes mentioned by the interrogators. These people all have families, just like us. They're human beings, for God's sake. It's not right!"

"Bob, you're taking it too seriously. It may just be Islamic propaganda. Let's relax and have a few *Mojitos*."

"Maybe you're right, I guess."

And we did, *Mojitos* in hand, snuggling together and watching the sun beat down on the silver sands from the high, blue, windless sky.

The days ticked by most pleasantly in the idyllic island, but the Guantanamo situation continued to nag my mind. I was deeply worried about the matter, and decided to speak to a Cuban friend in our hotel.

"Alex, what are the feelings of your people about this situation down in Guantanamo?"
"We do not want it and do not approve of what is happening there, but what can we do? They are doing it here to embarrass our government."

"But are your government not paid by the United States?"

"Yes, but Castro has never cashed any of the cheques. We want an end to the legal situation of the ownership."He replied, glancing nervously over his shoulder.

"There's no one behind you, Alex."
"You have to be careful. The ears of the government are everywhere in Cuba. You know everyone earns only twenty dollars a month in Cuba. And now all the tips in the hotel are to be pooled, because some are jealous of what we earn."

At least the Cuban government's hands were clean in this nasty business, even if they had paid informers among the people. And even if most of the people were unhappy with their lot. And who could blame them on twenty dollars a month? Yes, the Cubans had troubles of their own.

I strolled down the clean silvery sanded beach, and gazed across the greeny blue waters, and saw the small fleecy clouds piling up on the skyline, above the scattered white sails. I picked up a handful of the crystalline coral sand, and let it fall through my fingers like a porous hourglass. I wondered how long I would survive that kind of cruel psycho-torture. Not long. Looking up I saw the tall palm trees bordering the beach. And my thoughts immediately went to *that* song again. But this time the sky and the trees and the sun had an orange hue. I wondered how such inhumanity could be happening daily on this beautiful, unspoilt island.

And I wondered what *Jose Marti* would say now if he knew what his homeland, so lovingly immortalised by him in words, was being used for. And I wondered if any of the many singers in Cuba, and America, and all over the world, who sang the haunting" *Guantanamera* " refrain, ever thought about it, when they were singing the words. And I wondered what Pete Seeger would have said, if he had known, all those years ago in Dublin. And I wondered…….

A Faraway Place

The Arabian sun was beating down on the red sand dunes with all the heat of June, as the plane angled it's descent onto Dammam airport. She felt a tingle of excitement as she looked through the cabin window. There were large circles of green dotted on the parched, lunar like landscape below, which intrigued her. The passenger beside her explained that these were farms growing crops in the desert, by means of water pumped up from aquafers below the earth, and sprayed onto the desert sands by the long arms of slowly rotating pivots. *Everything seemed possible out here.*

Annie Clarke took a taxi from the airport to King Faisal hospital, to take up her six month nursing contract. Her short blond curly hair, and long legs were well covered by her black *abaya*, as she stepped out of the taxi into the sun's white glare. The heat seemed to bounce off the dusty road and the large white hospital building. It was her first time to work abroad, but she was not awed by this. Many of her friends had done it. Great way to get rid of your credit card debts, too. In Ireland in the late eighties, there was nothing doing except high taxes. Her widowed mother was not happy to see her go.

"Sure why would you want to risk going to such a faraway place, with such strange names? What's wrong with living here?" Her mother asked.

"It's alright ma, don't worry. A short break will do me good, and bring in a few bob. I'll write to you every week. Don't worry."

She *knew* she had to change her life. She had just broken off with her latest boyfriend, after two year's together. Yes, I suppose that was a factor too. No regrets there. The relationship was going nowhere. No commitment, or prospects of any. Better to make a new start before it's too late. Not that she was in any way worried about being left on the shelf, at twenty six years. She *knew* she was attractive, and had never been without a boyfriend since her teens. She had been around and had some fun. Now time had moved on, and she wanted a mature person with whom she could have a responsible relationship for life. *And* fun too. Yes, it was time for decision and change. This was the start of a new era, even if a long way from her wet and windy home near the west coast of Clare.

She settled in quickly to the new work environment. The hours were long and hard. There were many different nationalities in the large maternity hospital. Some were local nationals, all men, who mainly worked in administration jobs, and most of them were bearded. Sometimes she noticed the locals staring at her as she swished by in her spotless white uniform. The reason for this, she was later informed, was her blond features, a rarity in those parts. She soon made friends with some other Irish nurses. Her closest friend was Lily, from Sligo, a short, dark, jolly girl.

"Yeh, I'm one of the longest here. Stupid me signed on for a year. To clear all the money worries. It seems like I've been here at least three years already. Anyways I've only five months to go, *and* I've had one trip home."

"Hey, it can't be *that* bad." Annie said.

"Yeh, there *are* some compensations, apart from the money, I suppose. There's an Irish dairy company sales depot just across the road from the hospital. There's a good few Irish lads working there. That's the hub of our social life here, at weekends. Only for that, this place would drive you wacky. You must come over on Thursday night this week. They're having a party for a new arrival."

"Yes, I'd like that."

She felt a nervous excitement that she could not explain on the night, as she donned her *abaya* before heading off with Lily to the party. She had on underneath, a low-cut blue mini skirt, showing off her fine figure. Her face and lips were carefully made up, and she was well satisfied when she checked out in the mirror.

The evening prayer call, *Allah Akbar,* crackled out on the tannoys, as they hurried across the road and entered the depot through a side entrance. She noticed Lily looking anxiously over her shoulder as they went in.

"What are you looking so worried about?" Annie asked.

"The *mutawa*. The religious police. Their spies are everywhere, watching the expat compounds to make sure there's nothing going on."

"Like?"

"Illegal boozing, or hanky panky between unmarried expats."

"And if they catch you breaking these rules."

"You'd be kicked out of the Kingdom faster than you could say *King Faisal*. Or worse could happen. I *really* mean it. I'm not jokin' Annie. I could tell you some scary stories, but I won't."

"Right, I get the picture." Annie bristled at the realisation that women were treated as second class citizens there.

The room holding the party was small and dimly lit, with shadowy alcoves. In one corner was a flat table where drink, all home brewed, was served. She tried the red wine. It was rough. Just like the terrain outside, she mused. But after a few mouthfuls, it began to taste better. The record player in another corner was belting out *Neil Diamond's* greatest hits. Soon the room began to fill up. She noticed a lot of the Irish nurses were there, and most seemed to have struck up friendships with Irish lads from the depot. Lily spotted that she was on her own, and came over.

"Annie, come with me, I want you to meet someone."

She followed Lily over to the bar, where a tall, middle aged man, with red hair, was standing, pint in hand.

"Paul, this is Annie from Clare. You're both the new kids on the block." Said Lily.

"Pleased to meet you. I'm Paul Egan, and I'm from Waterford." He shook her hand, smiling. Lily vanished into the shadows.

The night passed quickly and amiably. She quite enjoyed his company, and he was a good mover on the dance floor. And not bad on the slow, intimate ones too. She learned that he was just getting over a difficult divorce, after a childless, five year marriage. He expected to spend six months there as Marketing Manager, before a transfer to the corporate head office in Riyadh. They parted, agreeing to meet again same time the next week. It was midnight when she returned to the hospital with Lily.

"Thanks Lily, I enjoyed tonight."

"Good. Your man seemed nice. See you tomorrow. Don't forget to lock your bedroom door."

"I won't. He *was* nice."

After locking her door, she pulled back the curtains, and the bright moonbeams lit the room and shone onto her bed. Then she removed her clothes, and climbed naked between the cool sheets, and lay there thinking of the red haired man she had met, and had became attracted to that evening, until her eyelids hung heavy, and she dropped into a dream filled sleep. The next day she took pen and paper, and wrote her first letter to her mother, saying only good things about the place and the job, and also that she had met a nice Irishman named Paul.

They met every week from then on, except when he was away on business. It was during the periods apart that she began to realise that she was becoming very fond of his company, and missed him a lot. *He* also seemed to fancy her, she thought, and always bought her jewellery if he was away on a trip.

"This is a present for our first three months together." He said, giving her a pair of gold earrings, one night at the weekly soiree in the depot.

"Oh, thanks Paul." She replied, in delight and surprise, and hugged him, then kissed him hard and deep on the lips. She felt his arms embrace her tightly, and his fingers pressed into her flesh. They adjourned to the bar to celebrate, and later danced closely to Cat Stevens' *Oh Baby, It's a Wild World,* It was a hot and sticky night, and the moon was on the rise. They went outside. Many of the party had adjourned to the swimming pool, drinks in hand. Some were splashing around in the pool, in high spirits. She heard Lily's high pitched giggle in the tumult.

"Come on in Annie, it's lovely." Lily cried.

"I don't have any swimming suit."

"Neither have I. C'mon, it's dark, most of us have nothin' on 'cept a smile."

"Will you get in too?" She asked Paul.

"No, if you don't mind. I'll keep an eye on the clothes." He replied, sipping his drink.

The cool water on her limbs had a therapeutic, almost erotic, feeling. It was like a release from the daily repression she felt in the hospital. To hell with the *mutawa*, she thought as she floated peacefully on her back, eyes closed.

Paul held the bath towel open for her as she stepped from the pool. The crescent moon was high in the night sky, in it's back- to- front way, as he helped her dry off from behind, in the shadow of the depot building. She felt him kiss her on the side of her neck. A shudder went through her bones, as he whispered in her ear that he loved her. She felt his hands touching her through the towel. A wave of abandonment surged over her, before she came back to reality.

"No Paul. Not now. Not here." She grabbed the towel tight around her.

"Sorry, guess I got carried away. Love is like that, it carries you away. I love you, Annie, *and* I want to marry you."

"We'll talk about it again. It's after midnight. Got to go now." She mumbled, as she struggled back into her clothes.

They parted with a quick kiss. She found Lily waiting at the gate.

"You're late. What've you been up to?" Lily enquired.

"I'll tell you tomorrow. Let's get back."

They scurried over the moonstruck road, through the special side entrance of the dormitory, and then parted.

Annie's mind was racing with the words Paul had uttered. Did I imagine it? She wondered, as she flung her *abaya* on the floor, and lay on her back on the bed. He may not mean it. On the rebound after a failed marriage. I hardly know him, really.

She decided to have a bath before retiring. As she lay relaxing in the bubbly waters, she went back again in her mind over the events of the evening. After drying off, she walked back into the bedroom, lit palely by the moon's gleaming rays, draped her towel over a chair, climbed into bed, and closed her eyes.

Through her half- asleep eyelids she thought a shadow had come over the moonlight, and her eyes flickered open to check. She saw the large shadowy outline of a man looking down on her.

"What do you want?" She cried.

The man swore in Arabic, and pulled back the bedclothes, and grabbed her hair. She screamed, and tried to scratch his eyes and face, but only yanked his beard. He swore again, slapped and punched her hard on the face, and twisted her arms around before covering her head with a pillow. Then everything was black.

Her eyes flickered open for a moment, dazzled in the bright. In that instant, there was only a white ceiling, and a Filipina nurse's worried face looking down on her, before she slipped back into the dark. It seemed an age later, when she awoke again. This time she stayed awake, but had no feeling at all in her body. Did she just dream it? The Filipina nurse lifted her hand and felt her pulse.

"I'll get the doctor." The nurse left the room.

Within minutes, a man she recognised as the Egyptian doctor Mohammed Ashraf stood beside her bed. He too, felt her pulse.

"Good. It's steady. Miss Clarke, you have undergone a most severe and distressing experience. Apart from the physical damage, there could be mental fallout from the shock and trauma. You need complete rest for the next two days. You're in the right place, and all your friends are here, and will help you to recover. You are on painkillers at the moment, and I am prescribing further tranquillisers for the next few days, to help you rest. There will be no visitors in the meantime." He inserted a needle into her arm.

It was three days before she put a foot on the floor. She ached all over. In the bathroom she recoiled at the bruising on her face, when she looked in the mirror. O my god, I've two black eyes. She limped back to her bed, and cried. And cried. She felt unclean and tainted. Nobody will ever come near me now.

The next day the doctor informed her that she was fit enough to have a short visit from the local police, who wanted to ask a few questions. A short, swarthy man in brown uniform, with a pistol attached to a belt below his bulging waist, entered the room, and sat on the chair beside her bed. He was followed by two, tall armed guards, who stood on either side of the door.

"Captain Abdullah Karim. Madam, I am indeed sorry for what happened to you. I need to ask you a few questions." He said, as he sat on the chair beside her bed, and took a notebook and pencil from his pocket.

She said nothing.

"Can you remember what happened that night? I need your help to catch the person responsible."

"Yes, I can."

"Please describe what happened."

She said she had spent the evening with her friend Lily, and then said she remembered this large, bearded man, standing over her bed, before attacking her, and everything went black.

"Do you remember locking the door of your bedroom after you came in?"

"No....I... I don't recall." The captain looked up in surprise from his notebook, eyebrows arched.

He closed the notebook, and took six photos from his pocket and laid them on the bed. They were all of large, bearded, Arabian men.

"Do you recognise any of these, as the man who attacked you?" She stared at the pictures for a few minutes.

"No."

"Madam, this object was found in your bedroom. Is it yours, or do you know how it got here?" He produced a small, empty whisky bottle from his pocket. She stared in disbelief at it for a short time, before replying.

"No, I have no idea where it came from."

"Ok. I'll leave the photos with you. If you think you've seen the man in one of them, please contact me. Goodbye." She was sure she saw a look of contempt on his face as he stood up and left the room.

Lily visited her the next day. She told her about everything that she could remember, including Captain Karim's visit.

"Lily, I could see it in his eyes. He thought I got what I deserved, by leaving the door unlocked." She sobbed, as she spoke.

"Bastard. How dare he. After what happened to you. You poor thing."

She leaned over and put her head on Lily's shoulder, and sobbed deep and hard.

"Oh, Lily, I…I feel so helpless, and unworthy. I don't know what I'll do."

"Hush, don't worry, things will work out. They will, don't be fretting."

As Lily held Annie in her arms, tears began to trickle down her face as well. They stayed together in the room until the tears had all dried up.

Two days later, when she awoke, her mind was settled on what she must do. She realised that she must return home as soon as possible. She knew she would get no justice from Captain Karim. After having a shower, she dressed in her best skirt and blouse, but although applying heavy makeup to her face, was unable to mask the yellowing bruises beneath. Then she put on her high heel shoes, and sat in a chair reading a magazine, until Lily came for her daily visit. She explained her decision to her.

"You're right to go love. But I'll miss you terrible. And so will some others. When will you go? And what will you tell your mother?"

"I'll miss you too Lily. Promise you'll keep in touch. You're the best." She felt her eyes misting.

"I will, of course, I will."

"I want to go over to the depot tonight, and make my goodbyes. Will you tell them I'm coming? It may be awkward, but I have to face the world again. I'll ring my mother from there. The phones could be bugged here. Have to stop all this crying." She lifted a handkerchief to her eyes.

She wore her *abaya* up over her face until she found a shadowy corner in the depot. Everyone came over and said how sorry they were, and how they'd miss her. Conversation was stilted and short. She realised it was just as difficult for them to talk to her, as it was for her to talk to them. She felt embarrassed and awkward.

Her mother was delighted to hear she was returning for a short holiday. Annie put down the phone. She would explain things better when she got home. It wouldn't be easy for either of them.

Paul came over and said how shocked and sorry he was. He would kill the bastard if he got his hands on him. She realised then that he was the only one she really cared about.

"Paul, will you really miss me?"

"Yes silly, I told you I love you."

"Still?"

"Of course I do." He kissed her gently.

"Will you write to me?"

"Yes, yes,yes. Every week. "

He took a small box from his pocket, and handed it to her.

"This is for you. I was going to give it to you on your birthday next month."

"You shouldn't have Paul. What is it?"

"Open it and see."

She did. It was a diamond engagement ring. Her heart leapt.

"Paul, it's beautiful. I don't know what to say."

"Then say nothing. Keep it a secret until your birthday. I'll come over to you then for a few days. *Then* you can decide. Now is not the right time."

"No, it's not the right time. We should wait till then. You will write won't you?" She wiped away a tear, and kissed him lightly on the cheek.

"Of course, trust me." She left him then, and bade her goodbyes. Lily escorted her back to the hospital.

The next day, as the plane lifted away from the sun scorched runway, her thoughts turned homeward, and how she would explain things to her mother. And as the pilot fixed the flight path towards London, her spirits began to lift a little. And she began to think about her birthday. And if Paul would come, as he promised. And if he would write. Yes, that would be the proof. She would count the days for his first letter. And look out everyday for the postman coming up the road.

Decision

The old lady, grey haired and bent over, slowly made her way up the mountain path on her daily walk. She had a walking stick in either hand, and realised how much she needed their help, since her hip operation two years earlier. *Have to make it under your own steam. No wheelchairs for me,* she thought as she paused for breath, gazing over at Clare Island, bright in the watery mid morning April sunshine. *There'll be rain coming on the wind. Better keep moving.* Fifteen minutes later she reached the ramshackle barn, which was the destination of her daily walk. She stood there for a few minutes, her mind far away. She found an inner peace from her daily journeys there that she could not explain.

On her way back to Martin's house, she thought of the bad fall she had on the ice in February. She was afraid she would not be able to make her daily visit ever again. Happily she had recovered, but she knew that if she fell again, she would not be allowed to walk outside again. That was her biggest worry. *And what would she do then?* And then the answer flashed across her mind like a ray of sunshine on a cloudy day. She would stay inside the house, but she would still have her memories, and her dreams. *And she would dream............*

The golden autumn leaves were illumined an even deeper hue by the rays of the setting sun, sitting on the ocean's rim halfway between Inishturk and Clare Island. Kitty Lavelle pushed hard on the pedals to make the brow of the hill. Then it was all downhill, with Croagh Patrick in the distance, to the stone shack that was the local dance hall. She loved the feel of the wind in her hair, as she freewheeled down the mountain path. *Free like the birds.* The grazing sheep were startled as she rattled past on her old jalopy.

She went into the small house opposite the dance hall and parked her bike against the wall. There was still half an hour to go before the dance. Time to change into her blue dress. Her best friend Bridie Staunton would be arriving soon by bike from Louisburgh. As he touched up her lipstick, Kitty saw in the mirror a woman, still attractive in her twenty ninth year. She brushed back her fine head of thick auburn hair, and secured it in place with several clips. She had a boyfriend, John O'Malley, on and off for the past two years. He was a carpenter. No prospects in Ireland for him in the nineteen forties. DeValera's romantic vision of comely maidens dancing at the crossroads had just led to the emigration trail to England for the young people of Mayo. As John often said *"It takes a lot of that to fill a pint"*. He had told her at the dance last week that he was thinking of heading off to London, with a few pals. There were jobs aplenty over there with *McAlpines* and the like, what with the re-building after the war. And good money too. Enough to buy a house and get married. Not like *here*. Kitty was a primary school teacher in Tallaghbawn. She loved her life, in this wild place of great beauty. And her family and friends. And the dancing. She loved to dance above all else. Since an early age she had won medals for Irish dancing. Money isn't everthing, she mused. But she now realised it was time to make a decision about *her* life. A big decision. A noise at the door broke into her daydreaming.

"Bridie, there you are at last."

"Yes Kitty, I got a puncture halfway here."

"Did you have to walk here then?"

"No. I was rescued on the road by Michael Lyons on his tractor. He dropped me here and said he would fix it, and bring it with him later to the dance."

"Good for him. Men have their uses for sure. He'll get a right ribbing coming on a ladies bike. I suppose you'll owe him a dance then."

"I suppose I will. He needn't think he's getting a leave home though."

Bridie put on her dancing shoes, and started to powder her cheeks, peering into the small mirror inside the lid. Then she turned and spoke.

"Kitty, I've been thinking things over. I've finally made up my mind. I'm going over to Hull. I'm twenty five, and it's now or never. There's lots of Mayo people over there. There's nothing happening here. There's plenty of work there. Will *you* come too, Kitty? Oh, I would love it if you would. *Please* say you will."

"My god, but you're a great one for the surprises. And when would you be thinking of going? And what about your parents? Who will look after them?"

"In three weeks Bridie, I'll leave. My cousin lives over there and he'll arrange accommodation, and help find a job for us each. My young sister Sharon is still at home, and my older brother lives in Louisburgh. My parents will be looked after, and I'll be back and forth. Are you on?"

"Give me a few days. You've hit my head for six. I need to think about it a bit."

"Bridie, will you check if the seam in my stockings is straight at the back, and that there's no ladders either." As she puckered her lips in the mirror to check her lipstick

"You're fine Kitty, you're fine."

The room had started to fill up, and the air was filled with the excited chatter that Kitty loved, just before the dance started. Her head was reeling from what she had just heard. She could hear the music rising from the hall across the road. The Fay brothers were already in session. She waited a few minutes for Bridie to finish her cosmetic touches, before they both crossed the narrow path, paid their sixpences, and entered the dancehall.

The oil lamps spread around the hall, threw long shadows against the wooden lathes under the corrugated roof. There was a square wooden dance floor in the middle of the hall. Men grouped on the left side, as in the church. Ladies on the right. There was a log stove beside the little bar that served minerals and cigarettes. Sean and Michael Fay were seated in a dark corner away from the door. Sean played the drums and sang. Michael also sang and played the accordeon and fiddle. They were both bachelors in their forties, married to their music. They knew what the dancers wanted, and gave it to them every week. A mixed bag of tunes and songs, old and new. Kitty liked how the shadows played across the hall and dance floor. They gave an eerily intimate feeling to the hall. And a feeling of privacy when things got hot and heavy at the end of the night. And bodies were close. And offers were whispered in ears. And lips sometimes kissed. And sometimes more.

They walked across to the bar, and bought some loose cigarettes. They lit up and stood at the stove, surveying the scene. This was a good spot for dancing, as it gave the men the chance to ask them if *they* could heat them up on the dance floor.

"Good crowd here tonight, Kitty. Can't remember it ever being this crowded."

"Yes, a few new faces too. It might be the football final in Killgeever. I'm going to dance the buckles off me shoes tonight. I feel it in my bones. I feel it's going to be really a night to remember."

After a while, John O'Malley crossed the floor asked her to dance. It was a slow fox trot. They moved slowly to the music and into the shadows at the edge of the dancefloor. He pulled her close, leaned over, and whispered in her ear.

"Kitty, you're looking something special tonight, me little girleen."

"Oh go on, you'd say mass if you knew the latin."

"I would too, if t' would only win your heart."

"Flattery will get you everywhere."

"Let's go outside. The moon is shining full tonight."

"Not yet. I know what you're after. Let's keep dancing. I want to dance the night away." She moved in closer, and put her hands around his neck.

"Kitty, you're a right tease, but there's no one in this hall I'd rather have my hands around."

"Hard luck then. It's the Walls of Limerick. The Fay brothers have struck again. Spoilsports."

After the dance she met Bridie outside.

"Great night Bridie. Did you meet Michael Lyons?"

"I did."

"He brought your bike?"

"Yes, he did for sure."

"And did you have a dance with him?"

"I did too. I'm black and blue all over. He still thinks he's driving a tractor when he's on the dance floor. We bumped into so many people."

"Well, I don't suppose he's leaving you home then?"

"Well, yes. We got on well apart from the dancing. Would you look at the way he smudged my lipstick? And what about you and John O'Malley? You couldn't see daylight between the two of you all night."

"Yes, sure I danced the hind legs off him. It's payback time now. He's cycling home with me. I promised him. He's a bit moonstruck tonight."

"Careful how you go then. Don't do anything I wouldn't do. And don't forget to let me know about Hull this week. *Please*."

"I can look after myself. Don't worry I'll let you know. Safe home."

When they pushed to the crest of the hill, John swung off his bike and propped it against a nearby gate. The full moon lit the landscape in a translucent glow and Venus hung low in the sky above the hill. A fox barked in the distance.

"Let's rest a minute, Kitty, and enjoy the view. A fag?"

"Thanks."

"There's something I want to tell you."

"And what would that be?"

"I'm leaving next week for London. Me and a few lads from Louisburgh. You know it's been on my mind these past few weeks."

"Yes…….yes, I do for sure. And sure why wouldn't you? It, ... it's a big decision."

"'Tis. I'll work and save, and when there's enough saved maybe you'd come over Kitty, and see what you think of life over there. Would you?"

"I…I would have to think about it. And I…I very well might go. Anyways you go over there first and make your fortune. Will you write often?"

"I will surely. Every week."

He threw the fag away, and placed his arms around her. They leaned back against the gate and embraced each other deeply. Bridie had never felt like this before. She felt her normal inhibitions slipping. And she didn't care. She was shocked back to reality by a loud moo nearby from a curious cow.

"John, that's enough of that. I've got to get home. We're up early in the morning. That bloody cow. Scared the wits outta me."

She got to her feet and straightened her dress, and hopped onto her bike, telling John to write soon.

"To be sure I will." He called after her.

She lifted the latch gently on the half door, after putting her bike in the shed.

"Is that you alannah?" Her aged, widowed mother's cried through the half open bedroom door.

"Yes, mammy, it's me."

"Did you have a great night?"

"I did surely. See you in the morning."

"Night and god bless, love."

"God bless."

Kitty trod the creaking boards into her bedroom, and closed the door. She lay back on the pillow, and saw the incredible whiteness of the moon on the windowpanes, and the stars twinkling behind like flickering candles. Her mind and heart raced with the excitement of the night. The dawn birds were beginning their din, when she finally fell asleep.

John was gone one month when his first letter arrived. It was a page long, and covered mainly the great time he was having. And how great life was in London. Plenty of pubs, and betting shops, and the football pools. And the weather was so much better. He *did* say at the end that he missed her a lot. A few days later she replied in five pages. The second month no letter. The third month Kitty gave up her job, and travelled to Hull to join Bridie.

There were no teaching jobs in Hull, but she got a job serving in a large greengrocer shop. She also did babysitting jobs at night to make ends meet. She preferred looking after babies to the day job. She liked to walk around the port and watch the fishing boats coming in with their catch. It reminded her of home. The people were friendly but she had trouble with understanding when they spoke too fast. *They* also had difficulty understanding her.

Her digs was a bus ride from Bridie. They met every week, and either went to the cinema or the pub. After three months she received a re-directed letter from London. In a half page John told her he had so many friends, he missed her, and how hard it was to save with the cost of living. She replied saying she was in Hull and might go down to see him in London some weekend. She would love to see the shops and the sights. And she had saved some money, although she sent some home to her mother every week.

The day she got the bad news is etched forever in her memory. The postman handed her a telegram. It was from her brother Peter. Her mother was seriously ill, and she must return urgently. When she got home the next day, her brother Peter met her at the door.

"Kitty, thank god you're here. But mammy passed away a few hours ago. Peacefully. She asked for you."

"Oh no Peter, please tell me it's not true."

He held her gently.

"I'm afraid it is, sis. Don't blame yourself. These things are decided from above. It happened suddenly. Nobody was expecting it"

"I should have been here. I let her down."

"Not at all. You have your life to lead. She always said you were *her* girl. And she appreciated the help you sent her every week."

"Thanks Peter, for trying to make it better." She dabbed her face as she spoke.

He led her into the house. She met her older sister Grainne inside, with her five year old son Martin. They embraced and went into the parlour where their mother was laid out.

Months had passed back in Hull. She woke every night with the vision of her mother being lowered into her grave at Killgeever, with Clare Island and the sea on one side, and the mountains rising on the other. And seagulls whirling and screeching in the wild sky. And the wind whipping the waves white. And the fleecy clouds fleeing above in the heavens. She was still racked with guilt, as she sobbed herself back to sleep each night. She vowed that she would be buried in the same place as her mother. This decision made her feel better. She was beginning to become reconciled again. She also realised how much she missed her home sod. When all's said and done, she thought, it's your own flesh and blood that really counts. She longed for the friendship of family. And cycling along the mountain path with the wind blowing her hair behind. And the golden beaches of summer, with the sun high in the blue sky, and not a cloud to be seen, and the sand hot beneath her feet. And the meadows full of buttercups. *And* she missed the dancing. *And* the dancing.

She had not heard from John in London for a long time. He must have known her mother had died. Why did he not write? She began to feel that the only way she was going to get to see London was with Bridie. One night in *The Rose and Crown* pub Bridie informed her:

"Kitty, you'll never guess who'se coming to live in Hull."

"Who?"

"Michael Lyons."

"Really, tell me more."

"He's arriving next Friday. He'll be staying on the next street to me, and he's got a job on the building."

"That's great news. Are you still keen on him?"

"Well, you never know. We get on ok. We've been writing all the time. Have you heard much from John O'Malley?"

"I have to be sure. He's a great man for the letters. I must take a trip sometime down to London to see him. Maybe you'd come too?"

"I'd love that Kitty."

But with Michael Lyons' arrival Kitty began to see less and less of her friend. And John O'Malley's letters from London became even more infrequent and shorter.

It was almost three years since her mother had died. She couldn't believe it. She was standing once more in windswept Killgeever graveyard, as they lowered her sister Grainne's coffin into the cold, wet soil. A heart attack. Suddenly. And her eight year old son Martin left motherless. And Grainne's husband Tommy now on his own. And the farm to be looked after. What would they do? Kitty's mind and body were numb with the shock. She shivered in the wind as the priest said the final prayers.

As the crowd filed out through the gate, she found herself beside Grainne's husband. She took his hand in hers.

"Tommy, what can I say? Can I do anything to help? With Martin and the farm to mind. I'm here for a while."

"That's kind of you Kitty. It's hard on me at the moment with the lambing just started. Martin is very fond of you. You could stay with us for a while in the spare room, if you like."

"That would be fine. I'll do that. Until things get settled for you."

"You've just taken a heavy load off my shoulders, Kitty."

"And sure why wouldn't I? Wasn't Grainne my favourite sister?"

"She was indeed. She always spoke highly of you."

"And tell me is the dancing still on every week in the hall beyond on the hill?"

"Divil the dance there's been there for two years or more. Didn't Michael Fay up and take a heart attack that left him paralysed. And a lot of the locals are gone. There's no work here for them. The weeds are growing up through the old dancefloor, and last year a storm half took the roof away."

"Oh, that's a pity. A terrible pity."

"But there's dancing in Louisburgh every week. A Ceili. And in the Summer there's horse racing on Carrownisky strand. And the travelling actors, they still come every year to play in the Church hall."

"Really? That's good to hear." Her spirits lifted on hearing this.

Two weeks later she wrote to Bridie saying she had decided to stay on indefinitely in Kilgeever to help rear her sister's only child. She also mentioned that she had heard locally that John O'Malley had taken to the drink in London. She also enclosed a letter for her employer in Hull. She realised that she was not now going to get married. But better that than Tommy having to emigrate to England, with young Martin in tow. *Yes, much better.* Her decision became a comfort to her in later years when the days of looking back came, and when young Martin's children became like her own grandchildren.

Reconciliation

    The tall, greying, slightly stooped, man made his way with the help of a stick onto the upper deck of the HSS car ferry. He hated the stick and often wished to throw it away, but as he made his way along the slightly swaying deck, he realised that it was now part and parcel of his life, like it or lump it. His left knee was the problem. Cartilage. Old rugby injury. Then too much cricket and tennis over the years. The wear and tear of life, he mused. He had refused to have an operation. He might have to review that decision again, in the future, he thought, as he tap-tapped his way over to the railing.

    As the ferry passed the Kish Bank lighthouse the gulls were circling and shrieking around the Howth cliffs on his right, and over to his left, he saw Bray Head in the distance lit by the May afternoon sun. A few misty clouds at it's summit gave the Sugarloaf mountain the look of a brooding volcano. Then Killiney Hill, then Sandycove with it's granite Martello Tower, and then the jaws of Dun Laoghaire's horseshoe harbour yawning ahead. As the boat entered the harbour he saw the rows of large boats and yachts moored at the new marina. A wealth that never existed when he and his wife Kathleen and their family had taken the mail boat to Holyhead, nearly forty years earlier. Everything changed utterly. For the better. He was glad now that he had decided to take the train and boat back to Ireland. He had wanted to come back the same way they had left the country, and reflect on the changes that time had wrought over the years.

    When the boat had docked, he shuffled off carrying a small holdall bag, and headed for the Town Hall at the bottom of Marine Road. He then looked across at the huge modern complex where the Pavilion cinema had been, when he grew up in Dun Laoghaire, in the time of the trams and the steam trains. He remembered the time he had gone to see the movie *Dracula* there, in the sixties. It was the Hammer version, and in glorious, gory technicolour, was terrifying audiences all over Dublin. He had gone with a girl he had got off with at a record hop in Sandycove Tennis Club, the previous week. Dammit, what was her name? She had long black hair, though. There was a B movie on as well. Laurel & Hardy in *Way Out West*. The queues were all the way out onto Marine Road. He remembered well the tall kindly usher named Peter, saying to the girls in the queue, to watch out as *Dracula* might be sitting in the seat beside them. This raised an excited scream from all the girls. Everyone roared laughing all through the Laurel& Hardy feature, as the indomitable duo got into one fine mess after another. The laughter was heightened by the known terror that lay ahead in the fangs of *Count Dracula*. Yes he had really enjoyed that night, especially when the girl held him close during the scary bits; and there were plenty of those. He wondered what ever became of her.

    He walked to the top of Marine Road and stood outside St. Michael's Church. Only the great spire remained of the old church after the big fire that happened years after he had left. He did not go in. He had stopped that kind of thing a long time ago. He remembered way back, as a teenager, going to the annual Mission week in the church. It was the Redemptorist fathers. Their special focus was on Hell, and Death, and the next world. On the night when the sermon was to be on this subject, he sat in the pew, his knees knocking in fear of the fire and brimstone words about to be uttered. As the priest entered the pulpit to give the sermon, a coffin (presumably empty,..then maybe not) was brought out onto the altar. The next day the queues for confession were a mile long.

    He crossed the road and walked to the Royal Marine Hotel where he would spend the night. When he was young, the thought of staying in a hotel like the Royal Marine was beyond a dream. Only stars like Laurel & Hardy stayed there. And now he discovered that Queen Victoria had also stayed there. Just the place to map out his plans and thoughts for the reconciliation meeting the following day. He liked to plan ahead. Without a plan you just drifted. He was not a drifter. He always knew where he was going.

    That night, after dinner, he went into the Hardy Bar, and ordered a scotch & soda.
    He sat down and took out a notebook and biro, and began writing out his notes for the next day. And remembering.

    It was just a few years after he had graduated from UCD with a Commerce degree that he first met Jack Nolan. They were both members of Pembroke Cricket Club in Sidney Parade, and played together on the third team. Jack was a useful off break bowler, and *he* was an opening batsman with ambitions of playing at a higher level. Jack was a carpenter. They both met their wives, Theresa and Kathleen, at the dance in Pembroke. The girls were close friends. Paul Russell and the Viscounts were playing the night they first got off with the girls. The Viscounts played there every Saturday night. *They* were a great band. The dances in the cricket club abounded with stories of maidens being bowled over on the cricket square, after being invited to come outside. The groundsman was apparently not amused as he would have to repair the damage caused by the ladies' stiletto heels, the next day.

He had fallen for Theresa at first, with her fuzzy blond hair, petite curves, and flashing blue eyes, but pretty soon he realised it was Kathleen that he really desired. Funny thing, Jack later told him that he had the same experience in reverse with Kathleen. Kathleen was tall, with auburn hair, brown eyes, and an elegant grace. The girls both served their time in the relationships making cricket teas in the summer months. They went out regularly on double dates, mainly dancing or to the cinema. He could hardly remember a time when there was a serious quarrel between the four of them.

A few years later, it was wedding bells time. Jack and Theresa got married first, and he was the best man for them, and Kathleen was a bridesmaid. Six months later, he and Kathleen returned the compliment to Jack and Theresa. Pretty soon children arrived for both families, and they gradually drifted apart. *They* had two girls and a boy, all under five years. Jack and Theresa had four children, two boys and two girls, including twins, in the same period. Jack and he both had good jobs, and were just about able to keep their heads above water with the bills.

Time passed without contact until they met by chance one Friday night in the *Graduate* pub. He normally had an after-work drink there, and was surprised to see Jack.

"Jack Nolan, if it isn't yourself. What'll you have?"

"Yes Joe Reilly, it *is* me, good to see you, old scout. A pint would do nicely." He looked a little haggard.

"Here, knock that back. What've you been up to these past few years?"

"Work, work, and more work. We've got six mouths to feed. It's not easy. As you well know yourself. You've got five. But you have a big job in an oil company. I'm depending on the building. Thank god, it's going well at the moment. Same again?"
Jack placed the empty glass on the table.

"Sure, why not, it's Friday. How's Theresa keeping? And the kids?"

"They're fine Joe. Thanks. Sometimes it can be difficult making ends meet. And how's Kathleen, and all yours?"

"In good health, thank god. Cheers. To us all." He lifted up his glass to his mouth.

"Cheers Joe."

After a few more drinks, he decided to tell Jack of the plan he had been hatching in his head for the previous few months. He leaned across the table, and spoke in a low voice.

"Jack, let's be honest, you and I are both struggling to make a living, and raise our families decently. It's impossible to make it here, with the high taxation, and the dodgy economy. There's only one way to do it."

"And what's that?"

"Set up your own business. It's the *only* way. Be your *own* boss. Make *real* money.
Instead of making it for others, make it for yourself."

"And what about the risks, for jaysus sake? And the capital to start the business?"

"I can arrange the capital with the banks. I can do a business plan. My idea is to open a few hardware shops. Cash business. Just what's needed in the market, with the building boom. We could be 50/50 partners. Are you on? I'm going down that road anyway."

"You've got the brains Joe. I'd like to think about it. I'll speak to Theresa. I'll come back to you."

"OK, cheers Jack. Here's to the future. Our future."

"I'll drink to that. Cheers."

The business started well and after two years they had three shops trading profitably. It was only when they expanded to seven shops that the finances began to deteriorate. The building boom had slackened off, and oil prices went through the roof. The bank foreclosed. It was unfortunate that they had personal guarantees for the bank loans. They both had to sell their family homes. Luckily he was able to get a good financial job in London when they emigrated. Jack was in a tougher situation and he struggled to make ends meet. Jack blamed *him* for the business failure. Said *he* had all the brains. Said *he* should have foreseen the financial problems. Said *he* had talked *him* into becoming a partner. They had not spoken since that time. God knows he had tried to contact Jack over the years, usually at Kathleen's instigation. But to no avail. Even time could not heal the bitterness of their parting.

Kathleen had discovered that the Nolans lived in Cumberland Street in Dun Laoghaire. She badgered him ever since he retired, until he eventually relented, and agreed to make a surprise visit to Ireland on his own. And here he was. Nervous as the next man in, in a cricket match. He knew it was not going to be easy, but he had an idea of how he could break the ice in the fiord that had developed between the two families over the years. He had brought a special present with him for Jack. He had high hopes it would do the trick for him. *Yes*, indeed he was sure it would. He lowered a few more whiskeys, and retired for the night.

In the morning he checked out, and walked down Lower George's street, patting the holdall bag to ensure the present was there. It was. He passed the M&S shop, where Woolies used to be. Then the red bricked St Michael's Hospital, where he had his appendix operation. Then up Library Road to see the old playground. It was gone. A little grey haired lady with glasses stopped beside him as he gazed blankly at the place where he knew the playground had been.

"Mister, it's moved. It's further up Library Road. Follow me an' I'll show you."

"Thank you. I was worried it was gone completely." He leaned on his stick, and followed her.

He looked in at the children playing in the new playground.

"We're all children at heart, you know. I played in the old playground too, when I was young." The old lady said, as she moved on up the road, slightly bent over by the shopping bag that she was carrying.

"We are indeed." He replied, and as he looked after her, he thought he remembered her from those days. Dammit, what was the name? Then he wondered why the town had such a small playground, with all the new prosperity on display in the marina. Maybe children's needs were not a high priority in this neck of the woods.

He crossed over the road, and walked back down, and stopped in front of the steps of the library. Thank heavens for Mr Carnegie. He remembered the many times he had walked up those steps, when he first joined the library, and the many times going to get books for his invalided mother. She enjoyed nothing better than a good book, and a cigarette.

The musty smell inside. The reverent, almost religious silence. The scolding for getting the books wet. Or sand from the beach infiltrating the plastic covers. And the late penalties. Agatha Christie, Zane Grey, Ellery Queen,, James Hadley Chase, Hemingway, Steinbeck, Hammond Innes, John Buchan, Patricia Highsmith, A.J. Cronin, Graham Greene. The Thirty Nine Steps. Gone with the Wind, Hatter's Castle, The Keys of the Kingdom, The Grapes of Wrath. And always Gone with the Wind. All the sports books. Don Bradman's Art of Cricket. All the war books. Pat Reid's The Great Escape. Yes, thank you Mr Carnegie.

He finally reached the house of the Nolan family. The black paint was flaking off the door. He checked the number with his notepad, inhaled deeply, and rang the bell. No answer. He rang again. No answer. This time the door half opened. A small,thin- faced woman, bespectacled, with wiry grey hair, appeared. She peered at him for almost a minute in silence.

"Joe Reilly? Is it you? After all the years." Her voice was curt.

"It is Theresa. I've been meaning to make this visit for a long time. But you know how it is. Time flies. Finally here I am. I made it. How's Jack, and all the family?" The door remained half open.

"The family are well. But Jack died two years ago." Her face was blank.

"I….I…I'm shocked. I don't know what to say. I'm terribly sorry, Theresa."

"At the end we often talked about the old days in Pembroke. It was the one thing that cheered him up. He often mentioned your name, and Kathleen's, the Viscounts and all that. He was unwell for a year before he passed away." He noticed a tear trickling down below her glasses.

"It must be very difficult for you here on your own." The door was still not open.

"Yes, it is. But the family are a great help. You never get over it. *Never*." Her voice quavered.

"I'm sure. You know you have our sincere sympathies and prayers. I suppose I better be going then."

"I suppose. Give Theresa my wishes. I'll tell Jack you called. He *will* be pleased."

"But….but you just told me he had died."

"Unfortunately he has. But he's still with me. I talk to him every day. *There* he is." She pulled back the door and pointed into the small living room, and there on the mantelpiece, at one end, stood a small urn.

"That's Jack? He's in that urn?"

"Yes."

"I…I just remembered, I brought a present for Jack. Here it is." He handed her a small box.

"What is it?"

"Open it." She peeled off the brown paper, and opened the little box.

"It looks like a tiny urn."

"It is. It's a replica of the Ashes urn. I bought it for Jack this year when I was at Lord's cricket ground in London. This is Ashes year."

"What's inside it?"

"Jack would know. He will understand. I'm sure he'd like it."

"Ashes to ashes…..mmmm. Would you like to place it beside Jack, on the mantelpiece?"

"I would really like to do that, Theresa. Thank You."

"You're welcome. Here it is then." She handed him the tiny object. He walked past her into the room, blessed himself for some unknown reason, and placed it beside Jack's urn.

"For old times Jack. Happy memories."

"If you want to stay here on your own for a few minutes. Or have a cup of tea?"

"Thanks Theresa. You're very good. But no thanks. I'll be moving on now. The boat will be leaving soon. Kathleen will write to you."

"That would be fine then. Goodbye Joe."

"Goodbye Theresa. Let's keep in touch."

"Yes Joe, let's do that." She closed the door.

He made his way back up the street to Marine Road. As he walked his mind was a jumble of conflicting thoughts. He could not think straight. This was not like him. He felt as if he had hit over the head by a cricket bat. He couldn't blame Theresa for being cool with him. But you can't turn back the clock. What's done is done. Still he felt the pangs of remorse and guilt. *Maybe* his visit would help to heal the wounds. She seemed happier when the two urns were together. Maybe *they* would do all the talking he and Jack had not done over the years.

He paused for a rest outside St. Michael's Church, and leaned on his stick, and was glad for the support it gave him. A foreign looking man in tattered clothes was playing an accordeon nearby. He fumbled in his pocket for some loose change, and dropped the coins into the empty box beside the musician. He then entered the church, and came out again nearly an hour later. He could not understand what impulse had come over him to enter the church. He could not remember when he had last entered a church to pray, under his own steam. But he felt now that a weight had been lifted off his shoulders. He had just had a long conversation with Jack Nolan. His first in many years. The one he had been unable to have in the house. He decided then that this was the first of many chats he was going to have with Jack. After all, they had a lot of ground to cover. Yes indeed they had. An awful lot of ground. He put his weight on the stick, and shuffled on down the road towards the harbour, and as he did so, he felt he was treading with a lighter tread.

Survival

The sun burned down out of a cloudless Arabian sky onto the blood red sands of the *Ruba Al Kali*, shimmering to infinity on the horizon. Pat Farrell switched up the AC in his Corolla Crown to full, as he sped along the straight, dusty road back to Riyadh. No wonder they call it The Empty Quarter, he thought, as he sped past the ruby ocean of sand. It's empty all right. No quarter given either. Nothing could survive this heat. Must be 130 degrees. He saw glimpses of white shiny animal bones half buried in the red sand. How long were they were lying there, and how they had died? Survival in this harsh land is no mean achievement. He looked up to see vultures circling in the sky. Then he saw the object of their attention. Below was the bloody carcass of a sheep being savaged by two other vultures. He felt an uneasy twinge in his stomach.

He should make it to his compound before nightfall. It was Monday. Barbecue night. When all the expats would arrive with their homemade brew and steaks to socialise. The norm in Riyadh. All social events held behind closed doors. Most of those living on their compound worked with Arabian British Bank. Pat worked in the marketing department of an Irish electrical company. He and his wife Grace had arrived a month earlier. They both agreed the weekly barbecue was a *must. There wasn't much else going on socially.*

As he reached the outskirts of the city the sun was sinking below the desert skyline like a giant bloody eye. He pulled down the shade inside the car window. He saw that many people had parked their cars at the roadside and were kneeling on their prayer mats, facing Mecca. It was *saladh*, prayer time. Farther out in the desert a goatherd was prostrated on his prayer mat as the goats wandered unattended around the sands. He felt moved by these sights. The scene seemed timeless from the bible.

As he drove near the military airport he saw rows of Patriot missiles lined up on the tarmac. They looked so much smaller than he had imagined, when he had seen them on CNN. They had given so much hope to all those in range of the deadly Scud missiles, which could destroy from over 3000 miles. The reality was the Patriots had caused more damage in Riyadh than Saddam Hussein's Scuds. If a Patriot hit a Scud, they both fell to earth together, causing *more* damage to the unfortunates below them. If they failed to hit a Scud, the Patriots eventually plunged to earth in a flaming mass, causing untold damage themselves.

"I'm home Grace."

"Oh darling, thank God. *At last*. I've been counting the minutes." She embraced him.

"Something happen?"

"Yes, darling. I was in the garden reading a book when a snake crawled through a flowerbed near me and up a tree beside the wall."

"What did you do?"

"What do you think I did? I screamed."

"And then?"

"I rang security. They came, two Filipinos, but the snake was gone. They searched high and low. They think it climbed the wall. I hope it did."

"Sorry I wasn't here. That was scary." He held her tight.

"Oh Pat, I don't think I'll survive in this place." She kissed him hard.

"Nonsense, you'll be fine. It's a learning experience. The snake was probably more scared of you than you were of him."

"But last week it was that huge gekko, that jumped out of the cupboard in the kitchen. Scared the daylights out of me. I couldn't sleep a wink all night."

"Don't forget they say if you have a gekko in the house you won't have any cockroaches."

"Pity they don't eat mosquitoes as well."

"Anyways, I better have a shower before the barbie. What are you wearing?" He threw his briefcase onto the sofa.

"I think I should go in a bee keeper's uniform to keep the mossies at bay. I'll just wear jeans and spray well."

"I believe the new deputy manager of Arabian British Bank, Geoff Plummer, will be attending tonight. Just transferred from Hong Kong."

"Really, I wonder what his wife's like?"

"You'll soon find out."

The first people they met at the barbecue by the pool were Jim Evans and his wife Jill. Jim was a middle manager in the bank. Pat liked Jim a lot. He had been very helpful and friendly in the early settling in days on the compound. They also shared an interest in cricket.

"Everything going well then, Paddy old chap? Care to try my latest brew? It'll most likely leave you gagging for the real thing. But out here beggars can't be choosers, drink wise."

"Sure Jim, why not? I'm sure it's better than my concoction." He sipped the full glass.

"Not bad. When did you make it?" He noticed the ladies slipping off to put on the steaks on the grill.

"Only a few weeks ago. Did you not hear about the *Big Incident* here on the compound last month? All stocks of booze were wiped out in a matter of minutes."

"No. What happened?"

"Chris Adams, the general manager of the bank lives in the biggest villa on the compound. Has his own pool. *And* his own private liquor, the real thing of course, as you would expect. Chris and his wife Tina had gone away for a few days break to Dubai. They had a young Eritrean maid named Sophie. Only sixteen years. The day after they left the villa, the maid was found drowned in their swimming pool."

"That's awful, Jim. Everybody must have been devastated. Poor girl."

"Yes, everybody was devastated, but not really about the maid."

"Really?"

"Yes, when the news got about, everbody was scared out of their wits that the police would search every house on the compound. So everyone, yours included, rushed home to pour all their home made booze down the sink, including Chris Adams' real stuff. Hellish bad luck for all of us."

"I'm sure it was. *And* for the girl. And did they search the compound?"

"No, but you couldn't take a chance. It takes a few weeks to restock. That's why the last few weeks at the barbie have been a little sober, old chap."

"I hadn't noticed. And did they find out *why* the girl drowned?"

"No. And nobody is too concerned, to tell the truth. They just go through the motions here. She was *Eritrean*. If it was a western expat, there would of course have been a complete investigation. As much as there can be out here. It's jungle law, you know. Everyone for themselves, and devil take the hindmost. Cheers." He lifted his glass, just as Grace and Jill came back with the steaks.

"Thanks ladies, they look delicious. Here, try a glass of our Irish red wine, chateau Patrick, should be a perfect combination with the steaks. I must warn you it's our first production batch."

"Mmm, not bad Paddy, it's got a good nose." Said Jim.

"And what would *you* know about wine Jim. You'd consume anything if it's liquid." Jill said, her eyes twinkling.

"Grace, Jim just told me the story of an unfortunate drowning on the compound last month, just before we arrived. Had you heard about it?"

She hadn't, and as Jill commenced to tell her about it, Pat turned to Jim.

"Coming home tonight, I saw all the Patriot missiles lined up near the airport. It must have quite difficult living here, not knowing when a Scud missile was going to arrive out of the blue."

"Too right you are Paddy. Bloody difficult time. Like the flying V2 bombs in WW2, old chap. Still, stiff upper lip and all that, you had to get on with it. We were issued with gas masks, and all sorts of emergency instructions for a Scud attack. Everything was restricted, but there was *one* thing we all agreed would happen, come hell or high water."

"And what was that?"

"The weekly barbecue, of course. Every week we held it in spite of the curfew. A big brass UK commander lived here in one of the large villas, so we got away with it. It lent a certain *frisson* to the evening not knowing if we were going to be bombed or not."

"And was there *ever* an incident during the barbecue?"

"Yes, once. To my eternal embarrassment. I was fairly sozzled, and had gone to the gents, when the warning sirens sounded."

"And then?"

"I donned the gas mask I had taken with me, and curled up in a foetal position on the floor of the gents, as per standing instructions, with my hands covering my head. I felt the terrible pressure people must have felt in London in the last war, when the bombs rained down from the searchlight sky. Waiting for the roof to come tumbling in on top of me."

"And?"

"Well apparently the all clear sounded very soon after, but I never heard it. Everyone adjourned back to the barbie, and the drinking and chat carried on. It must have been at least two hours before somebody started beating down the gents door. Obviously in a *desperate* way. When I opened the door, there was Joe Guthrie, who works in post department, holding his crotch. He told me the all clear had happened ages ago, and to get out of his way quick. Frightfully embarrassing old chap. I still get ribbed over it. And to nearly get peed on, or worse, into the bargain."

"You're still my hero. Even though disgraceful under pressure." Said Jill pecking Jim on the cheek.

"I'm sure the bank will reward the loyalty of all their staff in hacking it out under such difficult conditions."

"I sincerely hope so Paddy. Here comes our new second in command, Geoff Plummer, and his wife Sally. I'll introduce you."

"Pleased to meet you Paddy. Been here long?" Geoff Plummer said, as he put a large cigar into his mouth, and extended his hand. He was short, stocky, with dark horn rimmed glasses.

"Just a month here, missed all the excitement with the Scuds. Like to try my Irish wine?"

"Sure Paddy, try anything once. Thought you'd have *poiteen*. What brings you out here?"

"Money mainly. And experience. There's nothing much happening back home."

"Yes, of course, all that IRA thing. Bad show that. There's only one solution in my book for the Northern Ireland problem."

"Really? and what is that?"

"I'd build a wall through the North of Ireland, and put all the Catholics on one side, and all the Protestants on the other."

"A Great Wall of Ireland? I wish it was as simple as that, Geoff."

"It *is* old chap, you know. Sort out the men from the boys. A bit of tough action is what's needed. Say, your wine is not bad, Paddy. Not bad at all. I'll have another glass. Would you like to play a game of mixed doubles tennis during the week? Say Tuesday night?"

"Sure, Geoff. Splendid. Look forward to that." Pat reckoned Geoff was not a man to be crossed in any way. He excused himself then to look for Grace.

She had got on fine with Sally Plummer, but was a little worried when he told her about the tennis game.

"I may not be up to their standard."

"You'll be fine, don't worry."

Pat had a restless night. The image of a young girl face down in a swimming pool kept flashing across his mind. How did it happen? Accident or design? Did her family know how it happened? He would love to find out. Best not to get involved though. Difficult enough to survive here without delving into other people's problems. Anyway justice was a hard thing to find in Arabia. The rules were harsh, just like the climate. He woke at dawn, exhausted.

The tennis match turned out an easy win for the Irish. Geoff shook his hand over the net at the end.

"Congrats, old boy. A win for the Paddies. Just as well I don't do this for a living. Better get in more practice for the return."

"Thanks Geoff. Look forward to that."

Pat somehow felt there would *not* be a return game. Some people don't like losing. Anything. Although they had won easily, he had copped a few dodgy line calls by Geoff. And a few wrong score calls. And a tendency to play as many shots to Grace as possible. He decided to overlook these as it was a social game. And he felt that Geoff would not take kindly to being taken on in front of the ladies. He thought to himself, it's not bloody cricket old bean. Instead he said

"Let's adjourn to our place Geoff, for a drink or three. We've just got a new brew on tap."

"Jolly good idea Paddy, I could do with a drink and a cigar."

After a few drinks, Geoff's face narrowed, and he leaned towards Pat in a confidential manner.

"You know my position in the Bank, Paddy?

"Yes, you're second in command to Chris Adams, I believe."

"Right, but I didn't come out here to play second fiddle to anyone."

"Really?"

"Yes, I've been with the Bank all over the world for twenty five years. I've paid my dues. I will be *number one* here in two years."

"I presume Chris Adams is in agreement."

"Well yes, we have an understanding. He expects to move onto higher things in the group. I have some work to complete first."

"Well let's drink to that. Cheers."

By the end of June the annual mass exodus from the Kingdom had begun; with the arrival of the school holidays, and the scorching heat of the summer months. The weekly barbecue continued, although the numbers had thinned out. Pat and Jim were wifeless, as they had already departed home the previous week.

"Can't wait for the next two weeks to fly, and then it's back to the lovely cool rain of Ireland, and the green grass. *And* the Guinness. J. Arthur. Your only man."

"Me too Paddy. I've got tickets for the first two days of the Lord's Test. The Aussies are over this year, you know it's *Ashes* year."

"I do indeed. We *do* play a little cricket in Ireland. By the way have you ever been to *Chop Chop Square*?"

"No Paddy, not my scene really. Have you ?"

"No, but a couple of my work colleagues went last Friday. Just for the craic, you know."

"I don't know old boy. You'll have to explain craic to me later. What happened?"

"*They were pushed right up to the front of the crowd .There was over one hundred thousand there .The noise was like thunder. They had a bird's eye view of two poor Filipinos, and two Pakistanis, getting chopped . The victims heads were hooded. Every time the axe fell the crowd roared like at a football game. The blood poured into the gutters. The heads were displayed later on high poles around the square. The two Irish guys puked on the street."*

"Well Paddy, we too have a hatchet man in our midst here on the compound." Jim's eyes had narrowed, and a frown came over his face.

"What do you mean?"

"Well, it's pretty clear now that Geoff Plummer's role is to axe as many expat jobs in the bank, maybe all of those living on the compound, in the next two years. Paul Summers the currency dealer, who lives in one of the biggest villas, is the first for the chop. He goes next month."

"Why? I heard he was very successful. Made buckets of money for himself. And the bank. His children boarding at the best schools in England. His family must be devastated."

"Well, old boy, sometimes you can be *too* successful. Doesn't always pay to earn more than the boss. Especially if he lives on the same compound. Tongues wag around the pool. Yes, his wife is distraught, and *he's* in shock."

"So Chris Adams is behind it all."

"Yes, he pulls the strings Paddy, and Geoff Plummer is his puppet."

"What about Paul's contract? Does he have any comeback."

"Not really. Contracts are renewed annually. Out here you have no rights."

"And after going through all that trauma with the Scud missiles. It doesn't seem fair."

"You're bloody right it's not cricket old boy. Anyway, let's not get too hung up on it. Let's drink to the holidays. And the *Ashes*. Cheers."

"Cheers."

Grace met him at Dublin Airport. It was raining.

"I never thought I'd see the day when I'd enjoy the soft feel of rain on a wet Irish day." He said lifting Grace in his arms, and hugging her tightly.

"Yes Pat, a change is as good as a rest. You know I was just getting to like that strange place before I came home. It sort of *gets* into you. But really it's your friends that help you survive there. The wives on the compound are very supportive."

"I'm afraid you'll have one less friend when you return. The Summers are leaving next month."

"*Oh*, that's sad. I really liked Jane Summers. I'll miss them. I wonder why they're leaving. Jane always said they were happy here. And making lots of money. What will they do? Is Paul being transferred in the bank?"

"No. He just had a local contract. It's not being renewed. I believe Paul is setting up his own financial consultancy company in Kuwait. It's a big upheaval for them. But that's the way it is out there."

"But could that happen to us too, darling?" A pensive look furrowed her brow.

"Who knows? I don't work in the bank. *Luckily*. People come and go out here all the time."

"I suppose. It would worry you though." She hugged him tight.

When they returned to Riyadh, their friendship with the Evans blossomed. They sometimes went on weekend excursions into the desert in Jim's four wheel drive, when the weather cooled. Down the magnificent escarpment outside the city, along the remains of the ancient camel trails that brought spices and perfumes from the Orient across Arabia to Jeddah on the Red Sea. To see the fossils on the trails showing the whole place was once below the sea. To find old arrowheads in the sandhills. And desert diamonds rough among the sands. To see the desert eagles gliding high in the clear blue skies. And the shepherds tending camels and goats in remote, desolate places.

The next year passed fast. There was a gradual exodus of bank staff from the compound. Jim still remained. *And* Joe Guthrie, who ran the compound video library in his spare time. Some of his material was racy, and if discovered by the local police, he faced immediate expulsion. The other survivors mainly worked in specialist computer areas.

"Pat, I'm worried about Jim Evans. " Grace said.

"Why?"

"Jill told me he's under severe pressure at work. He's stressed out. And can't sleep at night."

"Yes, I noticed a change in him at the barbecues. He's not the perky Jim we first met. I wish there was something we could do."

"Maybe there is. Why don't you talk to him?"

"Well…..well maybe I will." He was worried about the change in Jim's personality in recent months. He guessed who was behind it. He found it a difficult matter to discuss with Jim. Not really his business. Men can be touchy about talking about such things. Better to leave it to Jim to bring the issue up.

The following Monday night at the barbecue he saw Jim alone, grilling his steaks. He approached him.

"Jim, I've been meaning to talk to you. How's it going for you? There's only a few of you left. Geoff Plummer's handiwork, I presume. You look a bit shattered."

"Yes, you're right Paddy. Last of the few. We're all dispensable you know."

"What about Joe Guthrie, the guy who runs the video library. *He's* still here. How come? He works in the post department. Surely he would have been one of the first to go."

"You're right. He was called to Chris Adams' office early on."

"What happened?"

"He was told his services were no longer required. But that night when Chris told his wife that Joe was going, she objected strongly. Said she couldn't possibly exist here without the video library. Joe was re-instated the next day."

"Well I'm flabbergasted. So that's how he survived."

"Yes."

"Jim, I wish there was something I could do to help."

"Thanks Paddy. Just talking to you has been a help. It's like the *Sword of Damocles* hanging over your head. I'll be glad when it's all over. Actually I have a crunch meeting with Chris Adams next Thursday. It could be bad news."

That night Pat tossed around in a cold sweat. He imagined himself in Jim's shoes. And he felt a pang of fear shoot through him. But what could he do? He racked his head for hours before drifting away into a restless sleep.

The following week he missed the barbecue as he was in Dubai on business. He couldn't wait to meet Jim the next week to discover the outcome of the showdown meeting. He spotted Jim quaffing a beer at the barbecue, and holding forth in conversation with a few people, while turning his steaks with the other hand on the grill. He doesn't look too despondent, Pat thought. But you never know. Grace spotted Jill in the distance, and went to see her. He headed in Jim's direction.

"Paddy old chap, how are you? Have a drink. Missed you last week. Let me put these blasted steaks to one side, and we'll find somewhere to talk privately. This compound has ears you know."

"I wouldn't doubt it."

They moved, drinks in hand, to a shadowy area near the swimming pool.

"Jim, tell me how it went. I can't wait."

"Well, I was called into Chris Adams' office about eleven o'clock on the Thursday in question, feeling like someone going to meet his hangman. Geoff Plummer was sitting there too, all smiles and friendliness personified. And on the other side Cecil Wilson the HR guy. *The Death Tribunal.* It was all palsy walsy stuff in the start, have a cup of coffee, talking about the state of cricket in England, and other blather, until I got fed up and asked them to cut to the chase and tell me why they wanted to see me, it was hardly to pat me on the back after my twenty four years service, as nobody had ever previously done so. They seemed slightly taken aback by my rat-in-a- corner-type attack. Then Geoff Plummer removed his glasses and started cleaning them, while he went on about competition in the market getting sharper, and how the bank needed to trim it's cost basis, and other such bullshit. I felt like saying to him, good, does that mean you're leaving, as you're a pretty big overhead yourself. I kept my counsel however, and nodded my head every so often, as if I completely sympathised with their predicament.

He prattled on in this vein for a while. The HR guy was silent throughout. Eventually, when Chris came out with the clichéd phrase that hard decisions had to be made, I knew the time to intervene had come. I said excuse me, I would like to speak for a few moments in private with Mr Adams. This completely nonplussed them, and after a few moments awkward silence, and a nod from Chris, they filed out the door a bit like sheep.I knew I had nothing to lose, and tried a little levity on Chris, asking him if the room was bugged. I got an icy stare in reply that soon dispelled any sense that this was anything other than a very serious occasion. Which indeed it was, but what the hell. I then handed him a sealed envelope, and asked him if he would like to read it's contents, before reconvening the meeting. He asked why should he, what relevance had it? I told that it would be in his own best career interests, and also the bank's best interests, to read it very slowly and carefully. That if the information contained in the letter got into the wrong hands, such as the bank's head office management, it would not do his prospects in the bank any good. Or if it got into certain media hands, the bank could be in hot water. Chris opened the envelope, took out the letter and read through the contents. *Twice.*

He then threw the letter on the desk, his face like thunder. Asked where the pack of lies contained in it had come from. I said that I could not divulge my sources, but that I felt out of respect for him (ha, ha), I should make him aware of what it contained. If the letter got into the wrong hands, there was no telling what might ensue. Of course I would do my level best to make sure that this did not happen. Unfounded rumours. The scourge of life in the Middle East.

I have to tell you Paddy old boy, I have never seen Chris Adams look so shocked. There was a look of panic in his eyes. Though I knew that deep inside, his ice cold brain was working overtime. Chris stood up and paced the office, his hands behind his back. Finally he sat down, and with eyebrows arched, looked deep into my eyes. I felt boring right into my soul. Said I was right to bring the information to his attention. Ill founded rumours could do enormous damage to the bank's reputation (and his). He said the letter was a libellous bag of lies, and he would consult his legal advisers regarding it's contents. He was going to suspend our meeting, square it with his colleagues, and instigate a witch hunt to find out the perpetrators of these scandalous insinuations. Asked also for my co-operation and discretion in the circumstances. I assured him he had that. And with that the meeting ended. End of story. After nearly three hours.

"Bravo Jim. Wow. You survived. Well done."

"Well, for the moment. "

"What *did* you say in the letter."

"I mentioned a few dodgy deals Chris sanctioned without proper authorisation from head office, to local Arab Princes. Cost the bank a pretty packet. But I think the crunch item was the information you gave me, Paddy. About the Eritrean maid drowned in his pool. That she was *pregnant*. That was explosive. Would have caused shock waves back in London. Picture the newspaper headlines. Not that Chris was in any way involved in the poor girl's demise. But he had the whole matter hushed up, used whatever pull he had locally. By the way, how did *you* find out she was pregnant?"

"An Irish nurse that I play tennis with, told me all the intimate details, when I informed her that the incident had happened on our compound. She had managed to see the medical records, as she worked in the hospital where the body was brought. And very nicely obliged by getting me a copy of same recently when I asked her."

"Anyway thanks Paddy. You *were* a great help. Couldn't have survived without you. However I'll start making my exit plans from the bank. *In my own time.* There's no way I'd stay any longer after what's happened."

"We're friends, aren't we? Happy to help. You know best for the future, I'm sure."

A few months later, Pat got the chance of a promotion and transfer to Dubai. When he told Grace, she was excited by the news.

"Great. I can't wait. They say the shopping is terrific there. Riyadh is not a place for a long stay. Still I'll miss Jill and Jim. They were true friends. And God knows you need them out here."

"You never said a truer word. Worth their weight in gold, good friends are."

That Time of Year

There was an early December crispness in the air. The last pale rays of light were fading, and early stars were starting to sparkle in the twilight sky over Dublin. The city was thronged with people bustling about to see what delights lurked in the decorated shop windows, delights that might entice them through the beckoning shop doors.

The tall, middle aged woman was early for her evening work shift in Switzer's department store, as she stepped down from the bus in Harcourt Street. She reckoned she had about one hour to spare. *Time to cross over to St. Stephen's Green, and have a smoke, before the park closed.* Her favourite seat was where she could see the ducks being fed. The seat was vacant, but the ducks were not there. *I wonder do they have a bedtime?* Looking up at the high flickering stars, she exhaled the smoke from her lungs, and felt herself slowly relaxing.

This was her favourite time of year, even if the workload was unending, and the money scarce in the depressed Ireland of the eighties. *The joys of being an unmarried mother, with two young boys. She was better off without him. Yes, she had loved him, but he loved the drink. Other women too. Could never hold down a job either.* They had lived in a rented two bedroomed flat in Rathmines, and struggled day in, day out, to pay the bills. Still she had loved him, and hadn't complained. Then one day, four years ago, he was gone. No word. Just upped and left. Not even a note. She had cried for weeks on end. Dark clouds of despair then slowly settled in on her mind. Six months in and out of the zombie land of a mental hospital came and went. Depression, they said, or some other medical name, she couldn't remember the exactly. Only that her mother had looked after the children, she would never have recovered at all. Or worse, the children would have been taken into care. That would have broken her heart. *Her mother was a saint.* She still had her dark periods, but she had learned how to cope. But there was something about this time of year that excited her. Made her blood flow a little faster. Made her heart beat a little quicker.

As she passed by the giant Christmas tree, towering at the top of Grafton Street, the Christmas lights suddenly came on, and everywhere was magically transformed into a wonderland of light and colour. Young carol singers with smiling faces were singing,
O little town of Bethlehem, How still we see thee lie, Above thy deep and dreamless sleep, The silent stars go by,……….. She listened for a minute, and was moved by the words, and the innocence in the faces of the singers. Buskers were playing further down the street, and mimers were performing, bringing smiles to glum faces. It was a fantasy world, evoking hope, and memories of childhood times. Reality was the ragged people begging at the street corners. And the pickpockets, and the hustlers out to make a buck, but she didn't really want to think about them.

She savoured the glittering atmosphere, walking down the tinselled, red bricked street, and began to think of the staff Christmas party coming up in two weeks in the Gresham Hotel. It was one of the highlights of her year, but last year Tom Gordon, a security guard in the store, had made it pretty obvious he fancied her, and had chased her all night. He just didn't get the message that she had no desire to ever again become involved with a man, and just wanted to be left alone with her girl friends. He had ended up ruining her night. *The nerve of him. Coming on like that, in front of all the staff, and management. I knew what he was after. But he was barking up the wrong tree.* She wondered if she shouldn't go to the dance this year. It would break her heart, and her girl friends wouldn't understand, but she didn't want to be embarrassed again.

She stood for a few minutes outside Switzer's window looking at the seasonal scene depicted there. It was *Santa's Cave*, with reindeers, elves, snow, and the Big Man himself, and presents galore. Scores of children were staring wide eyed into the window, as they queued to visit Santa. This is one of the reasons why I like this time of year so much, she thought. *Brings you back, it does. We relive our youth through the kids.* Then the annual dance flashed back into her mind. *Why should she not go because of that stupid man? Yes, she would go, and to hell with him.*

She walked through the shop door, feeling more confident after her decision, and headed for the cosmetics counter on the first floor, where she worked. As she passed the children's toy department, she saw that a lot of new items were on display, including a number of toys that she had never seen before. She knew any of them would be ideal for her boys' xmas stockings, and hoped they would still be there and she could afford to buy them when she was paid, at the end of the week.

The following Saturday her boys were playing a football match at their school, so she took the chance to slip into Dublin for a few hours shopping. The city was teeming with shoppers, as she left The Shopping Centre, and walked across to the children's playground in St Stephen's Green, laden with two bulging shopping bags. The wintry sun was shining on the bare trees in the park, as she sat down to watch the children play. She lit up a cigarette, and soaked up the happy scene. She had that wonderful feeling that she always got after shopping. Her spirits always seemed to lift at these times. She took out a hanky and wiped her forehead. A few beads of perspiration showed on the white cloth. She imagined that this was what an adrenalin rush must be like.

There was an assortment of children playing in front of her. Some dressed in tattered clothes, and others in designer labels. She wondered if the poorer ones were from the travelling community. A couple of the ragamuffin boys came near her, chasing a football.

"Hey, would you guys like something for your Christmas stocking?" She said as she put her hand into one the bags, and pulled out a small racing car, and a toy fire engine.

"Yes, thank you mam." They grabbed the toys and ran back to their friends, happy excitement beaming from their faces.

Pretty soon there was a procession of kids sneaking over to visit her, to try and cadge a free present. A half hour later she looked into both bags, and saw that of all the small things she had taken that morning, only two remained. They were to be for her two boys. *Mustn't forget them.* She now felt as completely satisfied as she had ever felt in her life. Not wanting to disappoint any children, she rose quickly and left to get her bus home.

A feeling of elation still persisted, as she sat in the bus, lightened shopping bags under the seat. It was hard to remember when she had started doing it, but she had to admit she was quite adept at this stage. *Must be years.* It was rarely anything for herself, or anything big. The trick was always to move around, and not become familiar in any particular location. *And never on your own doorstep. Never.* By sticking to these rules over the years, she had stayed out of trouble.

Another week passed, and the staff dinner was only days away. Whenever she spotted Tom Gordon in the store, she detoured to avoid speaking to him. Since last year she had consciously blanked him out of her life. This particular monday she was on an early shift, and decided to make a few last minute purchases in the store before leaving. She left the store, bags in hand, and started to turn left up Grafton Street. A hand descended firmly onto her shoulder. Turning abruptly she stared into Tom Gordon's clear blue eyes.

"Agnes, I've been trying to speak to you for weeks. But I get the feeling that you're trying to avoid me." His hand retracted to his side.

"Do you blame me after your carry on at last year's dinner? You ruined my night."

"Ok, you're right. I apologise. I was smitten, and got carried away."

"I think there was drink involved too."

"Maybe. Look I apologise. What do you want me to do? Grovel? I'll behave myself this year. Perfect gentleman, I'll be. I hope you're going to be there? And you'll dance with me, I hope too." There was a half grin on his face.

"I haven't made my mind up yet about going. And if I did, the last person I'd be dancing with is you." She spat out the words.

"Agnes, there are two small toys in your bag, which you took from the shop without paying for." He paused, and she froze, as the words sank in.

"I don't have to tell you how serious a matter this is, do I?" He paused again.

"No."

"However, maybe it's just the spirit of Christmas on me, but I'm not going to take this any further. On two conditions."

"And what are they?" Her eyes lit up.

"One is that you are to give the two toys to your sons as a gift from me. Say they're from Uncle Tom. I will pay for them by putting the money into the charity raffle to be held at the dance."

"And the second?

"You're to come to the dance, and be nice and friendly to me. Maybe even dance with me. Get the idea? Agreed?"

She hesitated for a full minute, before replying. Then stared into his blue eyes.

"Agreed."

The Hunt

The large man rushed up the stairs to change. He was late. Two things had delayed him. There was his weekly Sunday morning visit to Naas. She had been in a highly amorous mood that morning, and tended to his every need in a way that was both satisfying and touching. He enjoyed himself so much that he had lost track of time. She *did* remind him as he made for the door that it was their fifth anniversary. So *that* was the reason, he thought. Well, he couldn't deny the pleasure he had enjoyed that morning, but she needn't think the relationship would go any further. After all, he had two teenagers to deal with. And his wife Mary in a wheelchair, after falling from a horse four years earlier. He paused in the doorway, tucking his shirt in over his bulging belly, to say how much he loved her.

"Same time, next week, baby?"

"Yes, but I think the neighbours are getting suspicious. Maybe we should book into a hotel on Saturday nights, just for a change?"

"Maybe darling. Got to rush. The hunt starts in an hour. I'm late, and I've got a chore to do on the way."

On his way back to the farm, he stopped and parked his four wheel Jeep in the trees near the bridge that spanned the Liffey. As he neared the swollen river, he heard voices echoing from under the arches. He hid in the bushes until the coast was clear, and then disposed of his wriggling, yelping bundle in the muddy swirling waters. He then looked around to make sure he was not observed. He would have to make up a story for the kids and Mary.

   Putting his foot hard on the throttle, he switched on the radio. *Ticket to Ride*, by the Beatles. How appropriate. *Damn those people at the river*. He had lost at least ten more minutes. The song's lyrics reminded him of the Hunt. Yes, the thrill of the chase. He had to admit in recent times it was the excitement of the female company that he enjoyed most. He had also observed that during the post hunt drinking in *Burke's* pub, everyone seemed more turned on if the fox had been caught and ripped to pieces by the hounds, the blood flying everywhere. He did enjoy the blood. Gave him a high. He sensed the ladies did as well, although they tut tutted at poor Reynard's demise. That new rider at the last hunt was a real cracker. Jenny, he thought her name was. The sight of her bouncing astride a horse was more than he could resist. Ticket to ride indeed. And when after the last hunt, he had casually touched her in an intimate spot in the bar, she didn't bat an eyelid. She had turned quickly, and looked straight at him, with her blond hair, piercing blue eyes, and pouting lips. And smiled. He had smiled back. Then moved away. Never move in too quickly when stalking a prey. Wait patiently until the moment is right. Lore of the hunter. Today could be the right time. The thought excited him so much he nearly drove into the ditch, when rounding a sharp bend.

   After the song a newsflash on the local radio station said there had been a protest march that morning in the village against the blood-sport of foxhunting. It also said that a recent survey had shown a large increase in the number of under- nourished foxes scavenging for food in and around the village. The weather was to turn wet and misty later that day. *Damn do- gooders. Have nothing better to do. Damn foxes are a nuisance. Bloody vermin. We're doing society a favour. And preserving a worthy tradition too.*

He donned his red jacket and black cap, grabbed his whip, and rushed down to the stables. The stable hand informed him that his normal horse was lame. But there was a new grey horse, Jenny, just arrived that he could use. Jenny…..hmmm… good conversation piece for later, he thought.

"No time for trying her out. Saddle her up, and be quick."

When he arrived at the hunt's starting point the riders and hounds were well gone. He looked at his watch. *Damn it, they must have left on time. Probably due to the weather forecast.* He reckoned he had half an hour to make up. He knew the route, and reckoned he could catch up fairly soon. He clattereded off in the direction of *Glenasmole*, the horse's hooves sparking off the road.

Low mist clouds were hiding the mountains as he rode past the ruffled lakes into the shelter of the pine forests. The rain began to fall in a steady drizzle. The grey was by no means as fast as his normal mount. He worried that at this rate he might not catch up on the hunt. *Got to get a move on.* He whacked the horse hard with his whip, and raked his spurs into it's flanks, drawing blood. The horse reared up, and with a loud whinny bolted in a fast gallop. In the wrong direction. He held on, and lashed out again with the whip. To no avail. The horse was out of control.

After fifteen minutes hanging on, the mist had closed in, and he realised that he was completely lost. The rain was now steady and heavy. But the horse still galloped pell mell into the gathering gloom. A high stone wall with a tall oak tree on the far side loomed directly in their path. He realised the horse was not going to stop, so he used all his riding skills to help them clear the wall. Incredibly, the horse's hooves were a good foot higher than the stones as they sailed over. But he failed to see the protruding branch of the tree. It smacked into his riding hat with a sharp thud.

He felt himself floating serenely through the air like a bubble, before everything faded black. Then he was in a hot bath being rubbed down by a blond lady. She reached up over him to switch on the shower. The water cascaded down onto his face. Waking up suddenly he found himself lying on his back in the mud, rain spattering down onto his face. He wiped his hand across his forehead, and when he withdrew it, saw that it was caked in blood. The pain coming from his right lower leg was unbearable. His ankle was twisted completely around. *Definitely broken. And no sign of the bloody horse.* It was twilight and the mist had descended almost to ground level. Damn, he had no idea where he was. He searched inside his jacket for his mobile phone. It wasn't there. Damn, he must have left it behind in the rush.

Suddenly there was a high pitched whine emanating from under his body. He froze. The noise stopped. A few minutes elapsed before it started again. He finally looked down, and under his large buttocks saw the head of a young fox protruding, it's tongue hanging out. In a complete panic he grabbed it by the neck, and choked the remaining life out of the animal, before throwing it as far away from him as he could. *Jesus, he must have landed on a fox's lair.* He was trembling all over.

    In a matter of minutes a large fox appeared out of the gloom. It looked lean and underfed, with a long, mangy tail. It went over to the body of the young fox, and started sniffing it, before emitting a long, blood chilling bark. The fox then turned towards him, teeth stripped back, and looked straight at him, it's yellow eyes sharp and cunning in the dim light. Then he saw four more sets of teeth and eyes appearing out of the mist. The smell of fear permeated his body. Looking behind, he saw two more dog shaped creatures stalking him. He was surrounded. The noise of a river came from the bushes to his right. He started back sliding towards the river, to have some protection in case of attack. His hand fumbled over a small rock on the ground. Damn vermin, he shouted as he flung the rock, expecting they would scatter in fright. That seemed to the signal they were waiting for, and not long after, the screaming had died away. And the mound of teeth and tails had finished their chore. They then dragged what remains were left into the bog nearby, and waited patiently until everything had sunk out of sight. The pouring rain washed clean the red traces on the ground.

    A few weeks later, the local radio station reported that no trace had yet been found in the Dublin mountains of a missing huntsman. They also said that the search party were mystified to discover a small, shallow grave, covered with sticks, containing the remains of a young fox, apparently crushed, and strangled to death.

The End

    A bitter November wind from the east was blowing in off the sea. The tallish young man standing at the bus stop in Blackrock stamped his feet, and blew on his hands to keep warm. His mother had told him to wear his scarf and gloves, but he had ignored her advice. I wish she would stop treating me like a child, he thought to himself, *I've been working for three years now and paying my way, since I left school in 1960, but she can't change the habits of a lifetime. Bloody CIE, they're never on time, and the bus will probably be full when it does arrive.* A moment later the Dublin bound Dalkey number eight bus rounded the corner. He could see it was not full.

    He went upstairs, and sat in a seat as far as possible from the smoke haze, and let down the window a little, to allow some fresh air in. Normally he looked forward to Friday nights, after pushing a pen for five days in an office. But tonight it was different. Mags had been his steady girlfriend for the past six months, and he had decided to end the relationship that night. Why? No big reason. Just he was afraid it was getting too serious, and he felt it was too early in his life to become seriously committed. *There's lots of fish in the sea. Yeah, lots of them. And* the craic with the lads at the sports club.

    "Fares please." The conductor broke his reverie.

    He alighted at Nelson's Pillar in Dublin, and looked across O'Connell Street, at the large neon sign, McDowell's, The Happy Ring House. Don't think I'll be visiting there, for a while yet, he thought.

Mags was waiting, huddled in the doorway of the Metropole cinema, away from the biting cold wind. She had taken the bus from Rathmines, where she lived with her mother. She had a blue scarf over her long black hair. And a matching knee length blue coat, which showed her figure to fine effect.

They kissed lightly, and went on into the cinema. It was a light comedy *Move Over Darling*, starring Doris Day and Rock Hudson. It was passable stuff, but his heart wasn't in it that night, even when they cuddled and kissed in the dark. He had other things on his mind.

Afterwards, they went into Cafollas, and ordered two coffees. Although quite full, there seemed to be a quiet hush in the café. Mags spoke first.

"I really enjoyed the film. It's one of my favourites. What about you Jack?"

"Well, to be honest it was ok, but not my type, actually."

"*Oh*. You don't seem in good form tonight. Is something the matter?" She frowned.

"Well, now that you mention it, there is something on my mind."

The waiter just then placed two mugs of coffee on the table, saying at the same time.

"It's terrible news, altogether, isn't it."

"What news?" Jack said.

"You haven't heard." He sounded incredulous. "I'll turn up the radio, the ten o'clock news is on now. It's just terrible so it is."

The voice on the radio was coming from Dallas. President Kennedy had been shot, and was in a serious condition in hospital. Five minutes later, the worst was confirmed. The reporter's voice broke off in a sob.

They sipped their coffee in stunned silence. Minutes elapsed.

"It's the end of hope. I saw him in Dublin only last June." Jack said.

"Yes, I saw him too. So handsome. Now gone. It's the end of the light in the world. Now there's only darkness." She sobbed, and wiped her eyes with a hanky.

"The end of good, and the triumph of evil in the world." He sighed.

"Why, but why…"

"Nobody may ever know why. Such a shame. Such a waste."

"Jack, what was it you wanted to say earlier? She had pulled herself together.

"Oh nothing, it's not important anymore. Let's go."

They paid the bill, and walked out into the light of the cold and windy street .

The Well

I'm going down to the well for water,
To the cool well where water springs pure,
And echoes deep in dark, damp chambers,
Water music playing soft upon the ear.
Redemption in water, there I will find,
Washing away sins and cares of the mind.

And I will fill my empty bucket
To the brim in subterranean streams,
And I will see still water reflect
The sky's blue eye and my life of dreams.
Though stars fall down, and rivers go dry,
In my heart and mind, you will not die.

Cobwebbed store of heavenly teardrops,
Water of life to all living things,
Nature's own life blood that never stops
Flowing, fill my mind with imaginings.
I must not wait, nor even falter,
I must go down to the well for water.

The Mountain

I can still see you, proud, mysterious,
 Sometimes cloud shrouded, sometimes sun splashed,
Still, in a manner most imperious,
With sharp peak pointed ever skyward,
Like a crooked finger beckoning me,
To come and to become anointed,
With salvation waters streaming free,
From high, veined streams of the mind.
But I waited here on lower ground.

The west wind wild makes music of the soul,
Around your sharp stones, your rocky refuge
Of the mighty eagle in times of old,
Slain by man's hand in a manner savage.
You bid me come, you bid me look into
My soul, and into the face of heaven,
And be master of all places below,
Staying awhile in your craggy bosom.
But I stayed here, wasting passing seasons.

And though now I am old, still you stay young,
The years have not wrinkled your face like me,
Precious years of time have passed along,
Your song, forever young, it still calls to me.
As I stand here rooted to this earthen spot,
I hear it calling like an old refrain,
I wonder should I go or should I not
Go, where mist clouds tumble down with rain.
And I…. I will go now to the mountain.

Famine Grave

A heap of stones on a white sand shore,
Mangled shapes scoured by sea and wind.
Mute testament of a time no more
When death and hunger racked this land.
Lazy-bed mountains looking down,
Silent witnesses of your betrayal
By them, and those who served the Crown
With Judas greed and deeds disloyal
To you, left to a lingering death,
Alone in your leprous solitude,
Abandoned to your family and fate.
Neither man nor God was on your side.
Your silence loudly questions if I
Would have helped. I bow down and I sigh.

Eastertide 2005

Standing on the storm beach stones
The sun a bloody sacrifice
Slowly sinking to the edge
Behind the burning precipice
Beyond the sea and the sedge
Sends a quiver through my bones.

Redeeming the lost day and days lost
Not doing your will or anything
That might add to life or aid
Any human thing or being
Better the new life he's made
Following in your way of the Cross.

Rising again in a new world
Radiant rays of hope shining,
Far from my heaven's flaming
Blood canvas of heroes dying.
Your light in this world dimming
Reveals the meaning of your word.

Altar

On a road from flaming buttercup meadows,
To where the wild purple rhododendrons
Grow, abundantly in mountain shadows,
Far lands are linked in sad words like sad songs.
You stand set in a brambly bed of thorns,
A mossy monument, of memories borne.

Ancient before the Pharaoh's Pyramids,
No costly tombstone or worldly treasures,
To buy celestial passage to the gods.
Just an arrow wedge on modest chambers,
Facing the westering sun's declining flight,
Through cloud-flecked days into star-speckled nights.

Guardian of a place of Grecian beauty,
Barren beauty no oracle might describe,
Where sunken stumps protrude from their watery
Grave, drowned dead witnesses by your side,
When sepulchre was transformed to altar.
A carved cross is your stark reminder.

You've seen the silver sun's light come shining,
On boggy Doolough's yellow river land,
You've seen the skeleton Famine wretches walking,
To beg some food from the rich man's hand.
Then return, rejected, hungry and forlorn,
To die neglected in the raging storm.

Autumn Thoughts

On a rust-tinted October morn,
I walk a crooked woodland trail,
Wondering if the birds have flown,
While the mist lifts it's silver veil,
On life living, on life dying,
On leaves falling, on birds singing.

The harvest's in, the haggard's full,
Ahead are winter's darkened days,
Black bitter nights, when winds will howl,
And summer seems so far away.
Like the faded moon, my time has gone,
As here I walk, forlorn, alone.

Inside a twilight cathedral,
Of standing trees, and fallen trees,
Lies a graveyard quite surreal,
Of fallen leaves, and falling leaves.
My life is like a patchwork quilt,
Of times and places, and things heartfelt.

Times without number, I've trod this path,
Today I wander a way less worn,
Meditating life, contemplating death
In nature, and in a world stillborn.
I see silver cobwebs on the hedge,
Entangling death in gossamer threads.

In words we live, and in words we die,
Carved in stone on a lonely tomb
Stone, windswept beneath a dying sky,
Somewhere, fading under sun and moon.

Tide and time, they are flying so fast,
I must live this year as if my last.

Freewheeling

I'm freewheelin' down a mountain road,
Blooming all round, light is my load
Wildflower hedgerows flash gaily by,
Orange rimmed clouds, in an azure sky.

Whirring wheels gliding me along
A vista fairer than a song,
Where flower and weed intertwine,
In loving harmony divine.

Lark's birdsong in hovering flight,
Music of magical delight,
Banishing cares into the air,
Like smoke to slowly disappear.

Stacked turf ricks rise pyramid style,
Snowy bog cotton flakes there do smile,
Near a stony deserted ruin,
A haunted house where no life blooms.

Ahead a white sail on a calm blue sea,
Behind are dark clouds following me,
From mountain lakes and paths uneven,
But I'm riding on and into Heaven.

Over the Moors

I'm flying over the moors to you, Maggie,
Gliding past high mist clouds, and low green vales,
Over streams swollen, and mountains craggy,
In bright summer sun, in chill winter hail.
To a time and place in olden days
Faded now like the morning's haze.

And I will see you there as before,
Book in hand by the brass lamp's light,
Bellows blowing the stacked turf fire
Aglow, in dim dark shadows of the night.
The day ending in silent prayers,
Sacred Heart light glimmering up the stairs.

Music was all around then, a magical sound,
Radio days on battery charged wires,
Scratchy needles circling round and round,
Mesmeric circles on whirlpool lines.
I carry the cross of loss just for you,
I bear it constant, and I bear it true.

In Barrow streams, and never-fenced country fields,
We sported and hunted the long summer days,
And nights shot with glittering diamonds,
With the moon paling for the dawn of day.
You were waiting there when we came late home,
Reading and praying in your chair alone.

The special times when you dressed up in,
Your old fox fur and silver pinned hat,
Mothball perfume in the rose garden,
Freeze framed in a photo black and white.

I miss those days and I miss you sore,
You're in my heart and mind for evermore.

I remember clear when your light dimmed out,
I'ts branded so deep in my memory.
Running crazy along the road I felt,
Your spirit flash by me, at last set free.
So I keep flying over the moors to you Maggie,
For then, and for now, and for all eternity.

Yes, I Will

When pain's gnawing your aching bones,
And mad dogs prowl your darkened street,
Snarling at your hidden fear,
And you hide, afraid who you'll meet
From the shadows dark, unclear,
And panic is a rising moon.

On jungle roads and rolling seas,
In trembling trains and crashing cars,
White mountain journeys full of fear,
Or space ships sailing to the stars.
At home when you sit and stare,
At ravens nesting in your trees.

As the sun arcing the sky into
A coloured rainbow crown,
Or like an eagle soaring high
Above an arid desert plain,
Or like a beacon's flashing eye,
I will, yes I will, look out for you.

Two Angels

They came at night on wings of joy,
A bonny girl, and bouncing boy.
June arrivals, not unexpected,
Now starts life's love labour directed,
To share and to care, with loving hands,
Their every need and every demand,
Thru' all of the days, and the nights,
Thru all the weeks, and all the months.
And someday when you're aged with sleep,
Around your bed a watch they'll keep,
And you'll recall fond memories,
Of youth and joyful times like these.

Requiem for a Shop

Once there were eight, now there's but one,
Remains of the few, face of the past,
The doors soon will close for one last
Time, on a way of life dead and gone.
Rest in peace, your name's just a lost refrain,
And, Dear Departed, life will ne'er be the same.

Surely you remember those white smocked men,
Sharp knives in wooden scabbards at their sides,
Ready to wield and cut and more besides,
Whose blood –mottled aprons the faint –hearted frighten.
Serving to the end what you require,
Chopping on the block your heart's desires.

And do you recall the twinkle in the eye
Talk, while queueing on the sawdust floor,
And no one was rushing out the door,
Minds making up only on what to buy.
Parcelling your thoughts in brown paper wrapping,
An extra helping given for safe keeping.

 Dumb beasts herded lowing down the cowboy road,
The final round up in the sky, it's nigh,
Fear stalking the wind and the bloodshot eyes,
Destiny's destination about to unfold.
In a meat emporium, a humane goodbye
To life in green fields, under peaceful skies.

And who will preserve your memory?

And who will lament your fading away?
Oh, your time had come, they'll likely say,
Move on, progress, advance, that's be the cry.
Your memorial, it may be a restaurant,
Or a launderette, where clothes are sent.

Pompeii Days

The she- wolves howl all along the way,
As Vesuvius casts down an evil eye.

On days resplendent of the Empire,
Pomp and ceremony of triumphal arches,
The invincible army onwards marches,
Emperor gods, the people inspire.
Loving to live, living to love
In a way unloved from above.

Gilt chariots clattering on rutted stones,
Equine haste on sparkling hooves,
Odours rising from dank foetid grooves,
Beside sweet smelling shops and homes.
Gods of Love and War well respected,
In a proud world so well protected.

In the arena of life and death,
Man and beast stain the bloody dust,
Thumbs up,thumbs down, pay someone must,
With one last inglorious, dying breath.
Life and Death, who will wear the crown?
Gladiators plead, no mercy's shown.

In the theatre of the intellect,
No base desires appear to matter,
Spouting out words of endless chatter,
Plato and Aristotle command respect.
No blood lust here, only lofty thoughts,
Of life, and feelings that can't be bought.

The earth quakes an apocalyptic thundering,
A poisoned rain of deadly pellets falls,
Sleeping silent death for one and all,
The flaming torrents torment with burning.
The Eagle of Empire dead in ashen shroud,
Moulded molten figures dead upon the ground.

No more the she wolves howl along the way,
As Vesuvius still looks down with evil eye.

Years in Love

For two score years they grew in love,
Like flowers budding on a garden wall,
Or oak trees growing proud and tall
On a river bank in a blazing fall.

On wings of love they soared up high,
Into a blue and cloud free sky,
And birds were singing flying by,
Songs of love that ne'er fade or die.

Reaching out in love for each other,
Days turned weeks, months soon turned years,
Looking out for each other in ways sincere,
Each always wishing the other was near.

Tender and deep as the night was their love,
Like the moonlight in the sky above,
Lightly lighting the heavens serene,
A glittering, winking diamond scene.

Years have melted just like winter snow,
But you know the best has still to go,
Loving to live, living to love,
Beneath the sun, moon and stars above.

Alone

Staring thru an autumn window
Frosted grey in the Dawn's pale glow,
I see the yellow tender leaves,
Spiralling slowly in the breeze,

Waft to a rusted carpet shore,
Brushed by the wind for evermore,
Then vanish mysteriously,
Under silent skeletal trees.

Above are mossy greeny boughs,
Where no-one hears my silent sighs,
Black clouds cover the brightening sun,
Mourning early morning's gone.

Trapped by the sins of my past,
Fragile now in my house of glass,
Broken slivers cut sharp and hard,
Memories bleeding deep and dark.

Life is floating ever inwards,
Unlike the dead leaves on the sward.
Timeless days in my timeless room,
Endless suns follow endless moons.

The dead leaves will arise once more,
When Spring knocks soft on Nature's door,
While I slip down into the haze,
Clouding the passing of my days.

People are drifting all about.
If only I could just reach out,
And touch your mind and then your heart,
I'd pray to God for a new start.

Artist

I can still see him now in my mind's eye,
With his palette of paints of many hues,
By a lake where swans glide in elegant line,
Or on a seashore washed by white curving waves,
Alone under sun and indigo sky,
Brush strokes delicately transforming the view,
Reflecting that one clear moment in time.

He can colour the sky with a rainbow touch,
Darken the clouds on the sun's shining eye,
Blow the wind soft on a blue rolling sea,
Thunder the waves on a storm lashed strand,
With a flick and a dab from his magic brush,
Searching for something, he must try and try
Again, though it takes until eternity.

From the Holy Mountain

From the Holy Mountain I can see far,
With a hawk sharp eye through the mist dark clouds,
Clouding my mind, shrouding the sun's bright face,
To show me a land that shines clear and fair,
Tempting my soul fly from this hallowed ground,
To seek this mysterious, magic place.
Alone I will sail with angelic ease,
Over green fairy raths and wind –bent trees.

As I glide and float in the clear pure air,
Washed clean by the rain, dried soft by the wind,
I see drumlin whales in calendar enclave,
With a humpbacked island guarding their lair,
While the startled fishes swim in a fossil land,
Of bones and stones in a deep, watery grave.
 Wrack washed up on a kelp- strewn shore by chance,
Reminds me of my own insignificance.

From the Holy Mountain top I behold,
The sky all on fire at day's crimson close,
And the sun tumbling down the mountain's side,
Before Night's dark mantle begins to unfold,
And the moon glows bright in heavenly snows,
Till stars flicker out and the pale dawn arrives.
Memory is the garden of my soul,
I fill it with flowers as I grow old.

Like the Sunflower

How like the Sunflower turning and turning to the sun's burning face,
Each day, with petals opening and closing in some shining embrace,
Just like a moth around a flame, or a river flowing to the sea,
My ancient mind and body are drawn ever closer to thee.

And if his head lies long and low, saddened by the sun's no show,
He brings back the loss of a loved one left some long time ago,
And as he soulfully waits on the sky for that life-giving light,
My soul too is praying softly for the dark to become bright.

And if I cut him down and put him in a vase to gaze upon,
Would my life brightly fill with sunshine, like the golden-eyed one?
Or should I plant him tenderly in the garden of my mind,
To grow and show his shining happiness to all of mankind?

Lightning Source UK Ltd.
Milton Keynes UK
15 March 2011

169310UK00004B/11/P